Playing All the Odds

Playing All the Odds

Rená A. Finney

www.urbanbooks.net

Urban Books, LLC
78 East Industry Court
Deer Park, NY 11729

ISBN 13: 978-1-60162-251-8
ISBN 10: 1-60162-251-1

First Trade Paperback Printing April 2011
Printed in the United States of America

10 9 8 7 6 5 4 3 2 1

Distributed by Kensington Publishing Corp.
Submit Wholesale Orders to:
Kensington Publishing Corp.
C/O Penguin Group (USA) Inc.
Attention: Order Processing
405 Murray Hill Parkway
East Rutherford, NJ 07073-2316
Phone: 1-800-526-0275
Fax: 1-800-227-9604

Acknowledgments

God's timing is always perfect and he has chosen this time to allow me to reach inside myself and share another work to this literary arena. What a tremendous blessing. I'm not at all worthy, but I am so very thankful. All honor and praise is due the Almighty God for bringing out the best in me, even when I come up empty he continues to pour into my reservoir. Special appreciation and love to the man that stands by my side and who encourages me when I need it the most. You are my forever love and the man God created just for me. What a perfect soulmate you are. To my first born, Chanel who gave this novel a face. Thanks for coming up with the ideal cover at the last minute. Looks like my investment is paying off. You are my jewel, always know that. To Gee who reminds me to balance all that's on my plate of life and who encourages me to live life to the fullest, you are my anchor and always remember who you are and whose you are. Admiration to my parents, sisters, brother and the rest of my extended family for the roots from which I grow and the love we share that sustains me daily. Thanks to my sister-girlfriend Lisa Johnson who has been a constant. You remind me to soar above daily trials, sickness and when I think I can't go on, you stand in the gap and you remind me that I can. Where would I be without my agent, Maxine Thompson? She has pushed me beyond and cheered me on when I was close to the finish line. An abundant thanks is due you for helping my works come to life. Much love to my Urban family for all you do and for allowing me to be a part of the posse. To those who have become a fan and who have followed me during my journey and to those who are new to my works, please know that I write because of you and I'm constantly humbled to be doing what I do.

Be Forever Blessed!!! Rená

Chapter 1

Who would have imagined that after all these years she'd stumble upon him? As Fantasy stared at the image of the slender guy dressed in military fatigues, her stomach flipped and filled with something that was near foreign to her: butterflies. Here she was a grown woman who was supposedly well beyond the age of being blown away by a simple glance of the opposite sex. Yet, she sat glued to her seat in the stillness of the room, totally in awe of who she saw and, more importantly, what seeing him made her feel.

Fantasy was no giggling schoolgirl gawking at the cute boy in homeroom, so how could this sudden surge of emotion make sense? No, the woman she was now had progressed beyond the fluttering-butterfly-feeling stage. These days, her appreciative stare at an attractive man had matured to a settled glance, followed by a slight tilt of the head to access a proper full-body inspection. If that yielded a double take, Fantasy usually added a subtle, seductive smile, but not enough to make it blatantly obvious that she was at all moved by what her eyes were taking in. This little tactic wasn't a game, it was merely a learned trait, and despite discarding many of the things her mother dearest had taught her, this particular gesture had remained. If she had half a dollar for every time Valerie Whitman versed one of her self-proclaimed "living life" adages, she'd be able to live next door to Hugh

Hefner and the Bunnies. The one that rang louder than some others was something about games being played with terms that could be altered at will, and always, always adjusted to suit the high-stakes player.

Fantasy didn't start off as a high roller, but neither did it take her forever to change her status from the played to the player. As they say, she had "been there and done that," had the hat, the T-shirt, refrigerator magnet, and several mugs marking her emotional visitation to the wonderful land of love. There were just some things that she cared not to repeat; butterflies, being wooed, and the head-over-heels thing were three of them. She was, for the record, an honors graduate of the school of hard knocks, and here in front of her was a visual reminder in the adequate amount of pixels to make him much more than an illusion, or a figment of her yesteryear imagination.

The visual image was of the man credited with one of Fantasy's earliest lessons in love. There was a saying she'd heard countless times: "you never forget your first." She could definitely attest to that. Victor Charles had been her first, and this guy, the one on the screen, was definitely deserving of the rank of first. He had been the first one to take her for a romantic moonlight stroll, the first to listen to her dream out loud, the first to touch her soul with his words, and the first to knock it (her sweet spot) out of the ballpark.

Fantasy had always felt inadequate, like her presence did little more than fade into the backdrop. She considered herself a wildflower in a circle of attractive, sexy, and body-perfect college girls. And yet, the very first time they were in the quiet company of each other without another soul to hear his revelation, Victor told her that she stood out among her sisterhood posse. She thought she was barely average looking then, but, after that night and so many others, he reminded her that she was absolutely gorgeous.

The blessing had been that much had changed in her opinion since those days. Her body and confident persona were among those changes. Now, everything she was physically endowed with was in all the right places and in ample proportions. To add to her physique, Fantasy's cheeks held deep-set dimples, and her dreamy eyes seemed to tell a story that unfolded into an inviting pool of intrigue. With a complexion the color of warm caramel with a hint of chocolate, her skin was as soft as it was flawless. Her hair rarely had a strand out of place, whether she was on one of her "I need a change" sabbaticals and sporting a short cut, or wearing her usual above-the-shoulder hairstyle that effortlessly cascaded around her head. Either style made her fitting of any beauty or hair magazine centerfold.

She saw it all as simply her with nothing extra, even today, but he had seen so much more, especially when he claimed the most intimate and sacred part of her being. This guy was an expert at what he did; each time he touched her he was able to navigate to the exact spot. She remembered thinking after the first few times that her spot must have been marked with an X, because something deep inside pulled him there with little effort.

She couldn't help but smile as she thought about how he took his time with her. Each time, it felt as if he were creating a masterpiece, lovingly molding and blending something special between them. His level of precision was far beyond anything Fantasy's youthful mind could even begin to comprehend. What she did know was that everything he did felt better than good and beyond great. He stirred a hunger in her that could never be adequately satisfied. The truth was, Fantasy never wanted it to be, not by anyone else.

During those blissful months, he held an all-access pass with platinum privileges. In Fantasy's mind, all the time they spent together and the extra perk of giving so freely of all she possessed equated to him being with her for a lifetime. The lifetime commitment didn't happen, but what happened, thanks to him, was a broken heart. Yet, heartbreak aside, and if she sidestepped the pain, no one ever compared to Victor. He was more than attractive; from her first glance at him Fantasy thought he was drop-dead good looking. He had a smooth chocolate complexion with piercing dark brown eyes that could take your breath away. His full lips were absolutely kissable, and she would lose herself just by staring at him. Fantasy pushed her narrow tortoise frame Versace glasses up on the bridge of her nose and leaned forward, frowning just a little.

Fantasy was so close to the flat screen that she bumped her forehead. "Dag." Before she had a chance to register what she was feeling, a chirp alerted her that the front door opened, and her name was being yelled out.

"Fantasy, what's good? I thought we were going to lunch."

She rubbed her forehead while minimizing the screen, and pushed her chair back. Fantasy leaned to the side a little and waited patiently for her loud intruder to locate her. She was a little irritated at the interruption of her discovery, as her semi-cracked office door swung open wide, but quickly dismissed it.

"Nick, I'm sorry," Fantasy said. "I just remembered I was supposed to meet you at Jasper's for lunch, but as you can see I lost track of time." She looked up apologetically and touched the pile of papers next to her.

"Why didn't you call me?" She stood up and began putting some papers back in the folder, noticing that her hands were shaking. The image of Victor had unnerved her, and she took a deep breath.

"I did call a few times." Nick walked over to the desk, picked up her iPhone, and hit her passcode. The two shared everything, even private matters. "Sweets, it's muted."

Fantasy chuckled and reached for her phone. "Sorry, love. I forgot to turn the mute off. I only intended to work for an hour on next week's feature story, and, as I said, I completely lost track of time." She returned her phone to the desk and dropped down in her chair.

"So, I'm not important?" Nick tried to sound hurt.

"You, my dear, are very important to me. Don't even try to make me feel bad. You act as if this happens—"

"All the time. Yes, it does, and if I weren't your best friend I wouldn't put up with it. Not to mention I need to stay gainfully part-time employed by you."

Nick and Fantasy had been friends since graduate school. In fact, when she settled in Charlotte five years ago, he was between jobs and tagged along. It wasn't long before he'd landed a great job as director of production at a local news station, leased a condo, and settled into a nice, comfortable life. The area was growing, the industry was booming, and there were plenty of women to peruse in different shapes, sizes, and flavors. What was not to like about Charlotte? Whenever he and Fantasy were out and about, people often thought they were a couple, but friendship meant more to them than starting something that could end badly and cost them what they treasured the most. Nick was an attractive guy: tall, well built, copper tan, and as sexy as they come. He was the ultimate catch, and Fantasy knew that when he truly got tired of the bachelor's life, he would make that someone special a wonderful husband.

"And you love me, so I already know you ain't even mad at me." She smiled and tapped him playfully with the folder she was holding. "Why don't you go downstairs and fix us something to eat."

"Is that all I'm good for?" Nick picked up another folder, identical to the one she held, and began to look through it, acting as if he was ignoring the suggestion.

"I don't know. What I do know is I'm hungry and you know your way around the kitchen better than I. So, hit it, boy, and pull something together. Go work your gourmet magic." She raised her hand and snapped her fingers before turning back around to the computer. Fantasy smiled knowingly. He'd argue for all of two seconds about her taking advantage of him and his culinary skills, and in an hour or less she'd be feasting on a delicious meal in the company of her best friend. She started typing in a Web address and waited patiently for his playful retaliation.

"Because I love you, I'll pull something together. But don't think you are getting off that easy. It's jazz night at AJ's and you will be joining me." Nick stood against the doorframe and narrowed his eyes at her the way he always did right before he was getting ready to hit her with a dose of wisdom, which she always called, "the world and its affairs according to Nicholas Jamar Albright."

"Fantasy, you know I admire all that you have done and how you stay on the grind twenty-four/seven. I wish I were that driven, but there is life outside these walls and it doesn't include you jet-setting all over the place and writing beyond exhaustion, either. Forget that. How am I going to find the right man for you if you have no outlets whatsoever?"

"You ever hear of fate? That's exactly what will kick in when it's time." Fantasy spoke the words, but she wasn't completely sure that was what she was waiting for. She'd never done anything in her adult life on a whim, or with someone else controlling how a given situation would turn out. Never. It just wasn't her, but the reply sounded good, and, since it did, she would see if Nick bought it.

"You don't do fate. I know good and darn well you didn't think I was buying that. You'd think I'd get some credit for being your left and right hand. Seriously, Fantasy, I know lately any talk of the future makes you feel a bit out of control. Your career is going great, but your personal life, well, it's not as great." Nick paused, wanting to choose his words carefully. The last thing he wanted to do was bring to light the truth without the compassion he felt the situation warranted. "I know you, and I know you're ready for the next move in love."

"And you know all this how?" asked Fantasy. She wanted to take the high, playful road and not show the hurt the reality of the comment had on her.

"I know it's that way because it's that way for me too. Everything in life has an expiration date, all affairs a duration of time. We're such close friends and we share so much, and I believe we are both coming up on that time together."

"Tell you what, you go forth and I'll follow your lead." She tried to laugh it off, but Nick was right.

"Just so you won't have to sit here and keep coming up with colorful lies, I'm leaving the room." Nick chuckled, aware of what she wasn't up to talking about. "I'm going to see what's in the refrigerator and your overstocked pantry. Besides, there's a cutie I met a few days ago and she's meeting me at AJ's tonight. I need you to check her out."

"So, you want to use me?" Fantasy spoke as he disappeared, and smiled at the familiar practice of helping him with his femme process of elimination.

He was always getting her to check out one of his prospects. A few accepted that Nick's best friend was a beautiful woman, and others thought that they were friends with benefits. Either way, she'd give her two cents because he was like a brother and, while he joked and played, he was a great person and had a heart of gold. There was no way she'd let him be hooked by a no-account gold digger. She could spot "that kind" a mile away. After all, she grew up around that kind, and her recognition radar was still intact.

Fantasy already knew from the time he asked that she would go to AJ's for friendship's sake. She'd give his latest fling the once-over, peep what most men couldn't see and what another woman could recognize without taking a second glance. That would be her sole purpose for leaving the comfort of her home and a planned evening of doing nothing more than ordering Chinese.

This outing wasn't about her, so the most she expected was to enjoy a little jazz. It had been awhile since she had been out, so the soothing sounds of some mellow jazz would be a welcomed treat. She decided right then that she would savor the relaxation it would offer, and not think of work. No, there would be no research, interviews, or endless reports to sketch out and plan. For tonight she'd cast all of that to the side and rest. But, as much as she wanted to erase her recent revelation, unless her psyche did a serious 360, or she reverted to the time before her Facebook discovery, she would be thinking about Victor.

As soon as she heard loud clanging noises come from the kitchen, indicating that Nick was at work, Fantasy maximized the Facebook icon at the bottom of the screen.

"Victor." She spoke to the silence of the spacious but overcrowded home office. It was cluttered with every known tool of her craft, and, yet, despite what others would think of the disarray, it was to her ideal. Everything she needed was not more than a few steps from the oversized swivel task chair. Although the shelves were crowded, and books, folders, and files covered every span of space, there was still enough room to do a happy spin in the chair whenever a major project was completed.

Fantasy refocused on Victor Charles's page. It was week two since she'd joined the craze, and already she was logging into Facebook daily to see who had invited her to be a friend and who she recognized on someone else's page. The reports of this Facebook stuff getting a person hooked definitely weren't a joke or an exaggeration. She was putting in her share of time. Of course, it didn't help that she had inherited the nosey gene from her grandmother Pearl and was always up for any interesting information passed on. Whoever was telling their business—or someone else's, it didn't matter—it was all news to her, and like a regular National Enquirer reader, Fantasy wanted to know.

Today's Facebook discovery pinned her to the seat. The photo wasn't a clear one and she attempted to zoom in, but close up or not it was him, Victor Charles.

Looking at the caption under the photo, Fantasy corrected herself out loud with a tone of authority. "Command Chief Master Sergeant Victor Charles." Never in a trillion years had she expected this.

There was no need for further confirmation and yet she scrolled down and checked out his hometown, the high school and college he'd attended, and his military career. The final T was crossed when she rolled over the familiar faces of a few of his fraternity brothers.

She tried to smile slightly, hoping it would overshadow the melancholy ache that loomed deep within. The feeling lingered, and before she knew it she'd covered her mouth with both of her trembling hands and was staring, transfixed. Fantasy knew what she wanted to do, but she wasn't sure it made any sense, not after all this time. Before she could talk herself into it and cross over into a zone of uncertainty, she quickly logged out of the network.

"What are the chances?" she softly asked herself.

Chapter 2

The watch on Fantasy's arm displayed 10:47 P.M. It was an early evening, considering that it was a Saturday night. Those with the true intent of having a good time were in AJ's situated to enjoy the jazz music and exchange dialogue with the flow of people coming in and out. Nick took a sip of his Coke on ice and looked at her as she glanced around pensively. Dee had slipped away to the restroom, leaving the two at the table alone. "Don't tell me you're ready to go home." As much as it seemed that they and Dee had fallen into an easy exchange, and each appeared to be having a good time, he knew that Fantasy was working extra hard at it just for his benefit.

"I was thinking of calling it an evening." She showed him her impression of a sad face, knowing that he would be a little disappointed. She was totally disengaged from the club buzz around her; it didn't matter that several had asked her to dance, or that she'd had more than a few offers of drinks. A few overzealous men, who thought they were the epitome of God's gift to women, had dropped their business cards in front of her. "I don't want to rain on your parade, and please don't even think about leaving here with me." Fantasy felt out of place, like she was on the outside looking in. As much as the ambiance should have given her a happy feeling, there was emptiness. She hadn't told Nick because she knew he would have opened the friendship umbrella and they would have both been out together.

Nick stared at his friend for a moment before speaking. "Well, I take your early exit to mean that I picked well and maybe Dee has potential." He articulated each syllable of his last word for emphasis and laughed.

Fantasy laughed along with him. "You are so crazy." She beamed at her best friend's humor, yet she knew he wanted to know her exact thoughts concerning Dee. "You did pretty well." Fantasy wanted to be direct with Nick, but all of what she wanted and needed to share with him would take longer than the few minutes that it would take Dee to return to the table.

"Pretty well?" His right eyebrow rose slightly. "I searched every avenue, boulevard, road, and lane in Charlotte, not to mention the surrounding areas, and you give me 'pretty well.'" Of course, he hadn't been searching; his meeting Dee was something that had just happened.

Fantasy wasn't rating Dee as a ten. She rarely gave a ten-star rating to Nick's lady friends. Nevertheless, she wasn't exactly sure if Dee was more of an eight or if the high end of a seven was more fitting. "Nick, she seems really nice and she's a beautiful girl." She wanted to stop right there.

"And?" Nick needed a little more.

"Come on, Nick. I'll share the rest tomorrow, I promise." She paused for a second knowing she'd have to add something, anything to get him to give her a look of semi-satisfaction. "Okay, the fact that she can put two words together that actually go together is a plus. A few of your lady friends were challenged by the English language and the proper use of it."

Nick rubbed his goatee as if trying to recall. "Yeah, I do remember a few were a little challenged in that area."

Fantasy giggled. "I'm sure you do remember. But Dee's a far cry from any of them. She's a Sunday School teacher, sings in the choir, and helps feed the homeless once a week at her church's soup kitchen. And, as if that's not impressive enough, she's a guidance counselor at one of the magnet schools, owns a townhouse with no roommates—male or female—and there was not even a mention of a pet that would require attention. All of that definitely earns a check plus."

Just as Nick was about to push a little further, Dee returned to the table and slid in beside him. With an innocent smile she leaned against his shoulder, and looked at him with a stare of admiration.

Fantasy didn't miss the look, and she smiled at the two of them smiling at each other. She cleared her throat and reached inside her purse for her keys. "Dee, it was wonderful meeting you."

Dee pulled her eyes away from Nick. "Oh, you're not leaving, are you?" There was an unmistakable hint of sincerity in her voice that both friends noticed right away.

"I'm afraid that I'm a little out of practice with hanging out this late unless it's related to work." She looked at the couple and smiled.

"You need to work on that then." Dee leaned forward toward Fantasy. "I admire your drive, but from what Nick has shared and from what I sense, you need to relax more."

Fantasy was not offended at all by Dee's words. Honestly, she spoke the truth, and if someone she had just met could peep her hold card, she was truly wearing her life on her sleeve. "Dee, you are absolutely right. But, for tonight, I'm calling it."

Nick stood just as his friend removed herself from her seat. "I'll walk you out." He turned to Dee. "I'll be right back."

When they had walked a short distance from the table, Fantasy turned to Nick. "So you are walking out with me." She chuckled. "Why?"

"To say good night. Dag. Do I have to have any other reason than to make sure that my best friend gets to her car safe and sound?"

"You don't." She slowed down slightly and looked up at him. "But I'll save you. I like her. And because I know you so well, tomorrow when you call me bright and early, I'll share the rest. Deal?"

They were standing outside the entrance as a light drizzle began to drop from the sky. It made the forecast of rain apparent. "Deal." Instead of sealing their deal with a shake, he hugged Fantasy tight. "Love you and be careful. Text the minute you get home."

"I will, and I love you too, Nick." She moved away from his embrace, which was as familiar and comforting as an inhaled breath. As she turned to walk across the street, she turned once more and smiled at Nick. She could tell that, with Dee, something he hadn't expected was already happening. Along with the good things she planned to share, she'd tell him all about the look in his eyes.

Chapter 3

Fantasy walked around the front of her car and up the steps leading to the kitchen from the garage. She had already silenced the alarm from her keychain remote, so she opened the door and turned on the overhead lighting from the outlet positioned right next to the doorway. The house was so empty and seemed so much bigger than it normally did. Sure, she missed Kameron,that always went without saying. He was the apple of her eye and the most important person in her world. For twenty-one years she had committed her entire being to caring for him and assuring that he had all the love she could provide. Even though she was a single parent, he lacked absolutely nothing.

At his birth, when the nurse placed his tiny, premature, still-damp body on her chest, she looked into familiar eyes that were barely open and promised him all of her, and everything. She prayed silently that it would make up for who she could not give him, and at that precise moment she prayed even harder that it would always be enough.

That promise was easily kept. Fantasy would be the first to admit that her only child was a spoiled brat from the cradle to the present, but as spoiled as Kam was, he was a good person inside and out. He reminded her so often of her own grandfather, the only father figure he had growing up. Kameron's middle name was

Matthew, after his great-grandfather. The name was something she felt honored to bestow upon her son with the blessings of Matthew Whitman, who proudly told everyone that Kameron Matthew Whitman was his pride and joy. He had matured into a handsome, bright man with unlimited talent, a zest for life, and a determination to achieve all that he set out to capture, even those things that were slightly out of reach. Like his mom, he was an overachiever. The word "no" was not received, nor did he see it as the end of anything. Even in his relationship he was committed and so expressive toward his girlfriend Brittany; it was definitely not a trait of many young men his age. Fantasy never wanted him to display any character traits that could remotely mimic the man who was nothing more than a sperm donor. While she had no control over what he did or did not inherit, she was relieved that there were no telltale signs of her son being the love-them-and-leave-them type. If there had been one or even two who had suffered a broken heart from Kam, or retaliated as a scorned lover, she wasn't aware of it.

Her reality, now, was that Kam wasn't just two and a half hours away, which had always been comforting, but he was two weeks into a year-long internship in Washington, DC. He was in the thick of Capitol Hill among politicians, legal eagles, and the like, and she missed him terribly. It was a great opportunity for a law student, and receiving the assignment was beyond wonderful and worthy of a dozen kudos. From the time he shared the news up until she dropped him off at the airport, she celebrated with him. But the truth of the matter was that Kam wouldn't be right here in their home, or a couple of hours away, and, while she knew she was being selfish, that was exactly where she wanted him to be.

Fantasy kicked off her shoes, opened the refrigerator, pulled out a bottle of water, and looked at the clock again. Not wanting to think anymore or try to figure what had her in a twist, she reached for the cordless phone at the end of the countertop. She dialed quickly and waited for an answer.

"Hello," a deep, groggy voice answered.

"Kam, hey, sweetie, were you asleep?" Fantasy looked at her watch, wanting to confirm that it was just a little before midnight. Kam was a regular night owl. For him, midnight truly marked the beginning of a new day, and he embraced the wee hours of the morning as such.

"Yeah, Mom, I was." She could hear the familiar noise of him stretching. "But, no problem, I'm up just for you."

"Okay, what's going on? It's still early according to your body's clock." She paused and began to frown as her motherly instinct kicked in. "Are you feeling okay? You're not sick, are you? Is it your allergies?"

"Slow down, journalist extraordinaire." He chuckled. "Let's see. There is nothing going on. Yep, I'm normally still up and moving around. I'm fine, and, nope, I'm not sick. And I haven't had any problems with my allergies." He laughed. "Did I miss anything?"

"No, you did not, smartie." Fantasy rested her elbows on the countertop and adjusted her bottom on the stool that was positioned beside the island. "So then tell me why you are in bed so early. That is, if I'm not being too nosey." She added that as an afterthought. Kam often reminded her that he was twenty-one, and a grown man. It took awhile for her to adjust to the reality that her only child was indeed twenty-one. She never referred to him as a grown man because of the simple fact that she was still footing all his bills. Fantasy provided her only child with the finer things in life. The essentials she saw as "gimmes" or freebies. The extras that tilted the scale toward the elaborate side were much more than what he needed, yet she didn't mind nor had she ever complained.

Kam thought about giving her the "I'm twenty-one" speech, but decided it best to just provide his mother with the information she'd requested. It was either that or have her land on his doorstep. "Brittany came for a visit. I waited at the airport for hours because her plane was late getting in. By the time we got something to eat we were both exhausted, so we decided to turn in."

"Hey, Ms. Whitman." Brittany's soft voice could be heard in the close background.

"Tell Brittany hello." Fantasy was young once and she knew that half of what he said was likely true, but the part about being exhausted probably happened after they expressed how much they missed each other. She didn't even want to think about it. "Okay, well, I was just checking on you. Give me a call back sometime this weekend and have fun."

"I can talk awhile longer if you want, Mom. It's cool. I'm up now," Kam said.

Fantasy closed her eyes and could imagine how he was struggling to push his body into an upright position. His heart was in the right place, but, on the other hand, his body likely would not be cooperating. Waking him up from a sleeping state had always been a task, and getting him to focus on what was being said was an even harder one. "No worries, sweetie. I'm good, as you say. I love you."

"I love you too. Talk with you later." The phone line disconnected and he was gone.

Fantasy couldn't fathom why Kam's departure suddenly had her out of sorts this way. It couldn't possibly be empty nest syndrome; he'd been away from home too long for that. Then, there had been the fall right before Christmas, but she had recovered from the broken ankle months ago. Her primary care physician had warned that the pain meds and lifestyle adjustment of being confined to the house could have her off balance emotionally, but she was assured that once she had healed and was back to her regular activities that would subside. She waited for the emotional up and down, the sign of an out-of-control mental rollercoaster, but it never came. In fact, she worked from home, met every deadline, and remained on top of things.

With the help of her landscaper she even worked in her garden and added a few new flowers to the already colorful array of roses, snapdragons, pansies, and petunias. Not to mention, she had her grandmother and grandfather rush in for a week to do for her. Then, because Fantasy put up such a fuss proclaiming that it was merely a broken ankle and she could still function, she ended up being a second set of hands in working on a quilt and canning preserves. Kam and Nick added to the pampering by running around all over the city like crazy, catering to her every whim. Since she recalled the many times she had done for them, she allowed them to do for her and didn't contest it. But not one doctor said anything about post-accident emotional distress. So what the heck was this?

She had returned to her regular itinerary and travel schedule with no problem. Fantasy was in the air or on the road more than she was anywhere else, and that was pretty much normal for her. It had been that way since she accepted her latest promotion five years ago, once her son accepted one of the three offered academic scholarships. The new territory came with extensive travel and she was perfectly fine with that. Even when she was at home there were a thousand additional things that kept her busy. In short, nothing had changed about her lifestyle and all was as it should be.

She looked at the expansive area of her kitchen and the dark, merlot-colored breakfast nook that faced the rear of the house and overlooked the lake. Pausing right there and leaning against one of the chairs, she allowed her vision to pull in the view. As the moon shined over the lake it cast splashes of bright light over the ripples of water. She blinked, realizing how breathtaking the scene was. Her eyes widened at the beauty of it all. She couldn't remember the last time she stopped long enough to look out this window, or any window for that matter, to just take in all that was around her. Fantasy thought about the headache she had given the contractor when she had disliked the first five windows he had selected and installed. She had taken it upon herself to comb the inventory and special order availability of every window retailer within a hundred-mile radius before she finally picked out the perfect bay window. Now, as beautiful as the view through the bay window was, she couldn't recall sitting at the nook longer than the time needed to wolf down a quick meal, glance over some papers, or prepare a grocery list.

She couldn't remember either taking any time to seat herself at the patio that was located beyond the French doors off the kitchen. With all the fancy brickwork and the outdoor amenities, which made it perfect for entertaining, she could count on one hand the times that she had taken advantage of all that her money had bought to make even her outer environment lavish. There had been no planned event, or special summertime occasion, and, frankly, Fantasy hadn't even taken the time to entertain herself. Enjoying her home was something she hadn't really done lately, as much as she loved all that had been specifically created to satisfy her fancy.

To Fantasy it was home, to onlookers it was a mini mansion with all the amenities one could imagine. Everything was tastefully decorated, from thc pricy artwork to the furnishings arranged neatly atop the exotic Brazilian cherry wood flooring. The four bedrooms and the media room were covered with thick, plush carpet, the kind that could hide your foot with each step. The double front entry doors opened up to a large foyer with a cathedral ceiling and polished marble flooring. Nothing was out of place. Each section of the house accented the other in an explosion of beautiful colors that blended together nicely, creating an ambiance and an atmosphere made for enjoying home life to the fullest. It was a designer's envy. Of late, though, it seemed something was missing.

She looked up at the ceiling, as if looking for someone up there to converse with her and answer the question she spoke out loud: "When did I stop coming home?"

Standing up, Fantasy grabbed the bottle of still-chilled water, turned off the lights, and headed toward her bedroom. On her way, she passed her office, reached in, and turned on the lights. The office was a major contrast to every other room in her three-story dream house, it was her work area so she felt organized clutter was acceptable. She looked around, and while there was some work she could do, she wasn't up for it at all and looking down at her attire she wasn't exactly dressed to be sitting in front of the computer, working for hours. Fantasy decided that she would just check her e-mail and then she'd go to bed.

She hummed a tune she had heard earlier and waited as the computer came to life. Once it signaled that it was ready, she logged in to her e-mail and looked through a couple of messages. Her mind raced and she kept thinking about the photo of Victor. Then she thought about her conversation with Kam. Before she knew it, she'd logged into the Facebook network, put all her information in, and watched as her page came up. After a few minutes of skimming the page she couldn't take it anymore. Fantasy typed in his name and leaned back as his page came into view. Once it did, she looked at the photo, and the familiar feeling from earlier came over her. Fantasy's temple was moist with a light bead of sweat. What would she say to him? What could she say and why would she even bother? More importantly, what would he say? Would he even respond to her?

Before she could mentally argue the pros and cons, she clicked to send him a personal message. She cleared her throat and rubbed a hand over her hair. If she got to the end of the message and changed her mind, all she had to do was delete it and go about her business. Fantasy placed her hands on the keys and started a message:

This is a very distant blast from your past. I'm a very old friend from your college days. You likely don't even remember me, although I'd like to think we have a little history and I at least made a lasting impression. I really don't know what I expect or if I should expect anything, not even a response. I was looking at a page of one of your fraternity brothers, an old friend as well, and there you were. What a wonder this social network is; I just haven't determined if it's a good one or a bad one. I'm totally new to this, and I'm sure after a while I'll be able to decide. My intent tonight was to reach out and say hello for old time's sake. I hope all is well, Fantasy.

Fantasy sighed deeply when the last word was typed and her fingers became heavy against the keyboard. She couldn't believe that she had actually put the necessary words together to create the message.

She spoke out loud, "Now what?"

She was not one to have second thoughts. Normally if there was something she wanted to do, even if it was impulsive, she'd throw caution to the wind, carry it out, and think about the consequences later. As she thought about it, she realized that there really weren't any consequences here. He'd answer or he wouldn't; either way it wouldn't bother her. Fantasy reclined in her chair and placed her finger against her temple. As she allowed her head to fall back against the headrest, she closed her eyes, and immediately there was his photographed image. She had just looked at the one photo, but she didn't need to look at the rest of the album to know that the other photos would render the same feeling, the same looming sentiment. There would be no rest within if she stayed in this awkward place of not knowing if he would respond. The real question was: did he even remember who she was after all this time? Before she could pose another hypothetical question, she leaned forward just enough to read through the message again, and without letting another thought stroll through her mind at a slower-than-slow pace, she resorted to her old nervous habit of clenching her jaw. With a quick tap of her index finger, she hit send.

There, it was gone. She could not retrieve it or will it to return to her screen unsent. The message was there in his message box. Fantasy imagined that he would retrieve it, and, for the minutes it would take him to read and reread, the part of them that was ancient history would come to life. If there was any fiber of his being that recalled their past, there was a semblance of a chance that he would remember her. Remember them. If only for a moment.

Chapter 4

The restful night's sleep Fantasy thought she would have hadn't happened. She tossed and turned all night. At one point she dreamed a gigantic computer was chasing her. Just when she thought she had gotten away it tapped her on the shoulder and commanded that she hit send. As crazy as it was, the dreamlike nightmare seemed to go on and on. By the time the dark still of the night gave way to daybreak, she was wide awake.

Since enjoying her bed wasn't something she got to do as often as she liked, she didn't even budge. After flipping a few channels, she decided to partake in a little in-house church. The option was much better than getting up, dressing, and going to the New Life Christian Center: her second church home. She'd been going there forever and still she was listed on the church roster as a member under watch care. Fantasy willingly paid her tithes and offerings, and when in town she volunteered and helped out with the public relations ministry whenever she could. As somewhat of a journalism celebrity she even did a few speaking engagements and mentored a group of teenage aspiring media gurus.

Today, though, she didn't even feel like getting up. Maybe she was coming down with something. She just wasn't sure. Fantasy threw back the sheet and decided to go out and get the paper. She walked out of her suite, down the hall, and around the corner toward the foyer that led to the front door. It was mornings like this, when her knees didn't want to cooperate, that she was glad she decided to design her home with the master suite on the first floor. There were no other signs of anything physically wrong, but the familiar aches and pains had woken up with her. They were definitely not welcome, but they never ever asked her for permission to put a damper on her day. Nor had she received a warning that she would be plagued with rheumatoid arthritis which had gotten worse lately. Not to mention a painful herniated disc from an automobile accident a year before. Still, she pushed, and decided she would deal with it later, much later. That way she would be prepared for whatever medical advice they gave her this time around. Fantasy would listen, but she didn't plan on going along with nor giving consideration to any procedure they deemed necessary for a better-than-average prognosis.

She deactivated the alarm on the wall near the door and opened the front door wide, frowning against the bright sunrays. Everything was pretty quiet, but, then, it was barely 6:00 A.M. The houses on both sides of hers were occupied by two guys who, much like herself, had very busy careers. Both of them were single with no kids, and they always mentioned that there was no time for them to date and meet Ms. Right. They were too busy climbing the corporate ladder.

Fantasy's family track had not taken the traditional route. She was a single mother who birthed a son very early. Her grandparents insisted that she could be a mother, finish college, and go on to graduate school. With their help rearing Kameron, she jumped full force into the occupation of her choice, and the rest, as they say, was history.

Fantasy walked back through the route she had taken and placed her body back on the bed. Reaching for the remote, she turned to CNN, settled her back against two oversized pillows, and placed two small pillows under both of her feet. She was thinking that she should have detoured to the kitchen, turned on the coffee maker, and grabbed a bagel. Maybe later, she thought. She relaxed into the cushioning feel of her king-sized bed and allowed herself to become completely engaged in the world's current news events.

The phone rang, cutting into her news time. Process of elimination told her quickly that it couldn't be Kam or Nick. Neither of them would be calling before the sun had fully ascended over the day. There were only two people she knew of who got up with the chickens: Pearl and Matthew Whitman. Her grandparents were all for catching the early worm. Looking at the caller ID to confirm what she already knew to be true, Fantasy answered cheerfully, "Good morning, Nana." That was what she always called her grandmother. It was such a fitting term of endearment, and she loved the sound of it.

"Good morning, Fantasy. How are you this beautiful Lord's day?" Pearl Whitman's voice was as joyful and gay as it always was. As far back as Fantasy could remember, her Nana had never acted as if she had a bad day. She couldn't even remember an occasion that caused her to react any way contrary to her usual happy and jovial self.

Fantasy could hear the television and other muffled noises in the background. She didn't have to be in her grandparents' home to recollect the Sunday morning routine. Her grandmother would be in the kitchen preparing breakfast and finishing up Sunday dinner. Breakfast would be on the table by 7:30, and at 9:30 sharp they would be out the door and on their way to Zion Baptist. Because she could also clock exactly how long it would take Reverend Johns to share the gospel, they would be back home by 12:45. The two hour and forty-five minute span of time covered Sunday School, praise and worship, sermon, collection, and the after-service social exchange. Service time was so predictable, whatever the Lord told the good Reverend Johns to say he made sure it never took longer than thirty-five to forty minutes. He was old school, and felt that the yesteryear method of delivering a sermon was fine. In his opinion, the congregation didn't need a lot of extra hoopla, just the Word, one short hoop, and the benediction. "I'm fine. Just went to the front door to get the morning paper. Now I'm watching CNN and in a few minutes I'm tuning in to get a little in-house Jesus." Fantasy waited to see if her grandmother was going to chastise her for reducing Sunday worship to an in-house experience.

"Normally, I'd get on you for taking that route, but you have been working extremely hard lately. You really need the extra rest." Pearl responded to what her grandchild had shared.

"It's not my norm, but it's basically all I have planned for today." Fantasy leaned her head back against the cushion of the extra large down feather pillows, thankful she didn't get the lecture she expected. The idea of relaxing and getting the extra rest her grandmother had mentioned was just what she needed.

"That's a great plan. I wish we'd known you were going to take a rest day. Your grandfather and I could have missed service and driven up to spend the day with you."

"Well, I'm glad you didn't. Not that I don't want to see you guys, but that's a drive you two don't need to take on my account. I'm fine, and if anyone needs to be on the road to visit, it's me."

"Well, we are folks of leisure and can just about do whatever we want, whenever we want. By the time you do rest you are too exhausted to do anything. Hold a second, sweetheart." Pearl yelled out to her husband, "Matthew, check on the rolls for me, please."

"How is Granddad?" Fantasy glanced at the headline of the paper she had placed on the bed beside her. "I called to talk to him Thursday evening while you were at the nursing home playing bingo. He was so into some television show that we didn't chat long. You know how he is when he's watching one of his shows." She chuckled. Her grandfather didn't have many leisure activities, but watching television was at the top of his short list. He would watch everything from news, sitcoms, and detective shows to old westerns.

"Don't I know it?" Pearl laughed heartily. "Matthew don't talk to nobody when he's watching his shows. Not even me. I spend more time talking to myself than I do talking to my own husband."

"Got to love him." Fantasy laughed.

"You know I do," Pearl added.

It was always apparent that the older couple loved each other with a passion. Fantasy couldn't think of anyone she would want to spend a week with, let alone sixty years. Matthew and Pearl Whitman were stellar examples of the part that says "'til death do us part."

"Have you talked to Kam?"

"Yes, I talked with him last night for a few minutes. He's fine." Fantasy reached for the remote to turn the television down. She was trying to give her grandmother undivided attention, and yet the constant interesting CNN headlines were pulling at her. Fantasy muted the volume, knowing that it would make listening to her phone conversation a whole lot easier. There was so much going on in the news, all of the top stories were enough to distract anyone. "Brittany is there for a visit."

"Oh that's good. She's a sweet young lady; so polite and pretty." Pearl paused and coughed softly. "He's really taking their relationship seriously. She's the one, Fantasy. I wouldn't be surprised if we don't hear some wedding bells the minute he finishes law school."

"I've been thinking the same thing." She grimaced. Fantasy wasn't upset about that possibility, but it was something that she had not totally wrapped her mind around. She couldn't help but wonder if Kam getting married would affect their special mother-son bond. "Well, I want him to take his time. Even after he finishes school, he will need time to get himself situated financially. He'll need a house, a secure position with a firm, and a little mad money stored up. There's just so much to consider when you think about marrying someone."

"Those all sound like the logical steps necessary to walking down the aisle, but these are young folk; they don't always take the path that's clearly laid out for them. They'd much prefer some detours." Pearl had spoken out of wisdom. It was wisdom she had gained from raising her daughter, who chose a lifestyle so different from what she and her husband had expected. They knew she had a great mind and could easily have been a dynamic business person. They just hadn't expected it to be in the occupation she chose. Then there was their granddaughter. While Fantasy had a brief interruption in getting her life together, she'd been able to bounce back. Fantasy hadn't suffered. Pearl was sure that, whatever route Kam took, he would not suffer either. They had all pulled together and created a solid family for him, and he had flourished.

"Nana, you are right." Fantasy knew she likely sounded unsupportive. She really didn't mean to be all down in the mouth about Kam's relationship. Brittany was a jewel, and she was sure there were a lot of other females out there who didn't have it together like she did. The fact remained, though, that Kam was her baby boy. "Well, you go ahead and finish preparing dinner. I'll call you this evening, if that's okay."

"That would be perfectly fine. I'll tell you all about service and let you know how many people fall asleep during the sermon. I declare, Reverend Johns got to step it up a notch. I've been going around the corner to Bishop Thomas's church for Friday Night Live just to get my Jesus on. That man can preach 'em under the pews." Pearl cracked up, laughing at her own summation of Bishop Thomas's preaching.

"Nana, you are too much. Reverend Johns is going to catch you and that chasing-Jesus crew you hang out with. When he does, he's going to escort all of you right back to Zion Baptist." Fantasy was speaking of her grandmother's three best friends: Beulah, Sadie, and Martha. They were always by Pearl Whitman's side whether at church events, shopping, or just sitting out on the porch. They were the most lovable little ladies Fantasy knew. Not one of them looked a day over sixty, although they were each well into their seventies.

"He can't catch up. Our slowest speed is too fast for him. Now, I'll holla at you later. Peace out." Pearl hung up the phone.

Fantasy laughed, knowing that her nana had spent too much time talking to Kam. She spoke out loud, repeating Nana. "Peace out." It was time she talked to Kam about teaching his grandmother Ebonics.

"To think that boy is going to be a lawyer talking like that," she said out loud. He would often tell her that, regardless of what he did in his nine-to-five, he would always keep it real. She didn't mind the keeping it real part; however, she had a thing for speaking proper English on a regular basis. Fantasy always wanted people to know that she was well educated. It was a personal thing, perhaps, but she had worked hard to achieve a piece of the American dream against odds that were stacked against her. She felt it would be a disservice to her profession if she didn't articulate well. Now, of course she had a little hood in her; that was just the plain and simple truth. The streets of Brooklyn were still in her bones, but that was a world away. She had lost too much in those streets to hold on to anything that it had to offer.

Before she could put the cordless phone completely down, her cell phone went off. It was still early, and she wondered who it was until she eyed the display. "Good morning to you, bestie. Don't tell me you couldn't wait a few more hours for my report."

"You know I couldn't." Nick spoke with a husky voice that was laden with what sounded like the remnants of sleep. "I went to the bathroom to pee and thought I'd call before I go back to sleep."

"Hold up, TMI. I don't need to know where you just came from and what you were doing. Dag, we are too close." Again, Fantasy picked up the paper. All she wanted was a peaceful morning to read the paper and watch CNN. Her next plan of action would be to have a light breakfast of strawberry cream cheese on a bagel, and a cup of Jamaica Blue Mountain coffee with a splash of hazelnut cream. To make it all seem extra special, Fantasy thought she might even put the bagel on one of her good plates and use a matching cup and saucer for the coffee. "It's not like this is a new process for you. Same drill, just a different girl."

Nick turned over in his bed. "Stop delaying and give me the goods." Dee had spent a couple of hours at his apartment after they left AJ's. While they'd talked, and he'd held her in his arms, he was a gentleman and didn't even consider crossing the line with her. He never slept with a woman on the first or second date, and sometimes not even the third. That was a rule for him. He was old fashioned in a lot of ways. In fact, there were a few women he dated for a lot longer and he never slept with them.

"Okay, well can I at least call you back after I make some coffee?" Fantasy wasn't trying to buy time; she had no problem telling him about her discovery. The thing was that she was exhausted, and unless she took in some caffeine, she would be sleeping through the morning and most of the day.

"That won't work. We are on the cell and I'm sure you can chew gum and walk. So, waltz on into the kitchen and get your coffee and something to eat, all while continuing to talk to me." Nick hoped that Fantasy delaying the conversation didn't mean that her radar had picked up on something negative about Dee. It wasn't like her to be so indirect, and she was not one to avoid sharing when the situation was warranted. Nick added, "Stop delaying and just tell me what you think."

"Okay, jeez. You are so hard on me." Fantasy sucked her teeth playfully.

"Well, make it happen for a brother," said Nick.

"Can I at least brush my teeth and wash my face?" Fantasy questioned.

"If you can talk while you do it," Nick said.

Fantasy walked into the bathroom and turned on the light. "Nick, as I told you last night, Dee seems like a very nice person. I mean she's smart and pretty, and from all she shared, the lady has a lot going for her." She hit speaker and placed the phone on the granite bathroom vanity. Fantasy turned on the water and began to brush her teeth.

Nick listened to Fantasy's recap, but grinned to himself, thinking about her physical assets. There was a tightening down below, and he could only smile, thinking about the possibilities. He wasn't trying to make it happen immediately, but it was something to look forward to later. "She is so beautiful. I mean, I could look at her forever. The fact that she's got it all together is icing on the cake. To be honest, her looks and her body had me from the word go."

Fantasy listened as she placed a dab of foam cleanser in her hands and rubbed them together before smoothing it all over her face. "I didn't miss you checking out her body, but need I remind you there's more to consider? Nick, we have had our share of drama. I say 'we' because I've been along for the ride. And, let me tell you, riding shotgun with you is no joke." Fantasy looked at her face for a second before applying moisturizer to her forehead, cheeks, and chin.

"I can't debate that. You are a great friend, and, just because I know that you want to hear me say it, you've always been right there with me," said Nick. "I could sing a line of "That's What Friends Are For," but my singing voice doesn't kick in 'til noon."

"We both know you can't carry a note. Speaking of notes, Nick, do you remember Kelly?"

"Kelly?" he questioned.

"She was that nightclub singer you saw for about a hot minute. But, greater than that, she was the one who scaled the wall outside your apartment building and swung onto the balcony."

"Oh, man, how could I forget that trick? I still can't believe that someone so beautiful could be so out of touch with good sense. That crazy girl climbed over the balcony all because she had stood outside my apartment door and heard female voices. Number one: she shouldn't have been outside my door since she had not been invited; and number two: the voices were yours and Mom's. She just took it upon herself to drop by."

"You not inviting her might be what turned her into Spider-Woman. But as if climbing three stories weren't enough, girlfriend started a fire out there."

Nick recalled their shock at smelling smoke. Once they'd opened the balcony door, Kelly stood in the corner, holding a hammer in one hand and a rope in the other. "She almost gave my poor mom a heart attack. I got the lecture of a lifetime about bad choices."

"I remember." Fantasy was right with his mom about the bad choices. Kelly could have burned the place down. "You may have gotten a lecture, but Mom Albright almost knocked you down trying to get to Kelly. If your mom had gotten a hold of her, she would have had a beat down flashback every time she saw a match."

"No doubt." Nick laughed, thinking about how irate Kelly had been and how ghetto his mom had gotten.

She'd taken her earrings off and pushed her sleeves up. "Now, if you are finished going down disaster memory lane, let's get back to the subject at hand."

"All right." She paused. "There was only one small, tiny, weensy issue. I don't think that it's anything you should be alarmed about. To be completely honest, I almost missed it."

"What did you almost miss?"

"You remember how Dee and I went back and forth with the cosmetology conversation?"

"Yes." Nick was hoping that if he gave one-word replies, she would get to the point quicker.

"Her hair was perfect and flawless. But it was a little too perfect. I'm afraid to tell you this, but Dee wears a weave." She held her breath, knowing that Nick detested fake hair. He couldn't even stand seeing women sporting fake ponytails.

"What?" Nick sounded more awake than he did when their conversation began.

"It's a very expensive weave job and very high end, if that counts." Fantasy tried to add a positive spin to what he likely saw as doom.

"Dee's hair isn't the real thing?" Nick mumbled. If he had to pick one thing he liked about Dee, it would be her hair. Nick kept his hair cut short. A close inspection and anyone could tell that he had nice hair. If he were to grow it out, a mass of curls would have covered his head. He wasn't sure if his blessing in the area of hair was the reason, but he had a thing for hair. To him there was something erotic about running his fingers through a woman's hair. "Maybe it is her hair and she's mixed with something. Indian, maybe."

Fantasy poured the wonderfully smelling coffee into her "world's greatest journalist" imprinted mug. She mixed in a little hazelnut creamer from the container she pulled from the door of the refrigerator. Her morning relaxation had been altered to the point that she didn't even bother to remove her good china. "Nick, it's a weave. I don't think she has Indian in her blood. I could be wrong, but a brown-skinned Pocahontas she's not. In fact, I could pick up an identical match from one of the stores uptown." She took a big bite of her bagel that was covered with strawberry cream cheese, and waited for his reply. It came after a few seconds.

"Wow. I don't know what to say." Nick was blown away.

"It's just hair, and she never told you that it belonged to her." Fantasy was trying to help him see reason about something that shouldn't have made a lot of difference. "I mean, technically it does belong to her. She pays some good money to keep that hair looking tight."

Nick sighed into the phone. "Well, I'm going back to bed."

"Please don't tell me that you are kicking her to the curb because of her hair, Nick." She looked out the same window at the same view she'd taken in last night. It had been dark then, but now, in the daylight, it was just as beautiful. "That's not a good reason to stop seeing her. As I said, she seems like a really nice person."

"I know what I like, but I'm not that superficial or shallow, even when it comes to hair. I'll continue to kick it with Dee and see what happens."

Fantasy was a little relieved. The truth was, though, that no other weave-wearing female had gotten beyond hello with him. Other than the hair issue, which she knew Nick had a problem with, she rated Dee on the high side of an eight. It might not have been a ten, but it was a lot higher than her normal rating for his love interests.

"I'm going to bed now, and I'll get back up at a more acceptable waking hour, say around two P.M. Talk with you later."

"Oh, okay. Well, don't forget that I'm catching an early flight to Chicago on Wednesday and I won't be back until Saturday." Fantasy was mentally pulling together a list of what she needed to take care of before she left.

"No problem." Nick changed over to his professional side. "Handle your business and I'll have the research finished by Monday afternoon. Will that work for you?"

The last thing she was worried about was having the research on time. Nick was never late with his fact-finding investigations. "No worries. Monday evening is actually fine. I don't plan on doing anything with it until Tuesday. My plan is to rest and enjoy some solitude."

"Are you feeling okay?" Nick questioned, very concerned, suddenly hearing something other than exhaustion in her voice. Why hadn't he picked up on it earlier? She never just lay around when she was at home. Fantasy was usually as busy as a bee and constantly in overdrive. He hadn't put himself aside long enough to see that his friend was out of sorts. "Tell me the truth."

"I'm great. A little slow, but after I rest up for a couple of hours, I'll be as good as new." She hoped he bought her story. It was partly true. But saying she was great was a stretch. Fantasy hoped it fell under the category of a little white lie.

"Well, call me if you need me. I'll definitely check on you later," said Nick.

"You do not have to check on me later. Why don't you call to see if Dee wants to take in a movie? Or, better yet, take her to the park for a walk. That would be very romantic."

"Check this out: you telling me how to plan a romantic day. Like I'm the one out of practice." Nick couldn't believe his friend. She was always so concerned about what was going on in his life that she never paused to consider making the most out of her life.

"They tell me it's just like riding a bicycle." Fantasy started laughing. It was a strained laugh, because the truth was that Nick was right. She knew absolutely nothing about dating. In fact, her last date had been more than two years ago, when she'd decided that it was just too much work. It had nothing to do with attraction, or the gentleman not wining and dining her. Mike had been a good guy and he'd held his own. There was nothing that she could offer or give him. That was part of the problem: he wanted her and she couldn't risk being tempted to give herself to him.

"You know, there are a lot of people who fall off a bike." Nick busted out laughing.

"Ha-ha, very funny, best friend. For your information, I can still ride a bike. If you have skill, you seldom lose it. Now, bye. Go to sleep." Before he could reply, she clicked the cell phone off.

She had been messing around talking to Nick for so long that she was no longer tired. In fact, she was fully alert. Fantasy looked around. This was by far her favorite room in the entire house. Not because she was a gourmet chef; she was several perfected dishes from that. She could put together a decent meal that was not just filling but pleasing to the palate when she put her mind to it. Of course, her meals were nothing compared to the meals her grandmother prepared, but Kam never starved or complained.

Fantasy never wanted to be just average at anything. When time afforded itself, she worked hard trying to improve her culinary skills. On top of that, she spent a lot of free Saturdays shadowing her grandmother in the kitchen, hoping to pick up a few tricks of the trade that would make her a wiz.

For Fantasy, there was more to the custom-created kitchen being her favorite room than meal preparation. The kitchen was her grandmother's ideal space in her home. Nana's kitchen became a safe haven for Fantasy after her mother was brutally murdered and, at age twelve, she moved in with them. So many talks, comforting words, smiles, hugs, and kisses were shared to reassure Fantasy that all would be well. It seemed that fixing her heart became connected to creating aromas and whipping up an array of comfort foods that tasted wonderful and put an instant smile on her face. If her youthful metabolism hadn't worked so well, she would have been an overweight teenager. Her grandmother's method, coupled with all the love two people could give, healed her. Because of it, she survived a storm that would have so effortlessly enveloped her soul and left a huge hole in her being that no one could begin to repair.

She blamed her mother's demise on the lifestyle she lived, and she blamed her even more for making her a witness to it all. Valerie thought she was preparing her to take over the family business. She said it would make her tough, allow her to see life and living for what it was. A dog-eat-dog world, she'd say. She warned

Fantasy that only the strong survived and that if she wanted the good life, she'd have to take it. Valerie told her only child that her beauty was a gift from God and it should be used as a moneymaker. Fantasy didn't always understand all of what was shared with her. In time, she came to understand Valerie Whitman's measure of worth and what she believed to be the good life. She also lived with what it cost them.

Fantasy opened the pill bottle she'd removed from under the island. She swallowed two tablets and drank a little coffee behind them. Hopefully, the medicine would kick in and she would be able to do a few things around the house, maybe even get in a little shopping. Her weekly grocery shopping remained undone, and she had received some discount vouchers to her favorite boutique that she was dying to spend. A trip out would require the pain to subside, and she was hopeful the two tablets would work their medical magic. Not wanting to go directly to what she was doing before the interruptions, she walked into her office and turned the computer on. Once it came on, she logged in quickly to her e-mail account. She hummed while it came up, and she opened the inbox. There were a ton of e-mails; some would immediately go into her trash bin, and others were business and she'd check them out later. Just as she was scrolling through the inbox contents, she saw that a few people had sent her messages on Facebook. Julie Smith was one of her pending friends. She remembered her from an assignment she'd had a few years ago. Julie had also sent a wedding invitation some months ago. She'd check in on her later and see all the photos from what was probably a beautiful, breathtaking wedding. Fantasy didn't want to hate, but she was sure seeing photos of someone else getting married ought to do wonders for her spirits.

She went to the next message in her inbox that was alerting her that she had a Facebook message, and there it was: Victor Charles had responded to her message. After blinking a few times, Fantasy read the e-mail again. There was indeed a message from Victor Charles waiting for her. All that it required was that she log into the site.

He'd responded. It had been less than twenty-four hours. When she sent the message she wasn't sure that he would even reply. Now that there was a message waiting for her she wasn't sure what to think. Maybe she should have just checked out his profile and moved on. She was always the inquisitive mind when she should have left it all alone. Victor now knew that she was alive and breathing. Other than a few tidbits of personal information and a couple of headshots, there wasn't much he could learn about her.

After she glanced at a few other e-mails, trying to distract herself, she logged into her Facebook account. It took only a few seconds to go to her messages and open the one from Victor. Fantasy took a deep breath and began to read:

Yes, this is definitely a blast from the past, and a very pleasant one. I do remember you, Fantasy. I must admit, when I saw your message I looked out my window, thinking you had someone posted outside my house ready to take me out. You see, in remembering, I also remember the hurt I caused you. It was long ago, true, but nevertheless a period of time that I have not forgotten. I was young and dumb, and I handled "us" badly. For what it's worth, I'm so very sorry. Even now that doesn't seem like enough. I know my apology is coming some twenty years later, and I wish that weren't the case. Walking away from you was the hardest thing I ever had to do, and for all these years it has haunted me. Somehow I knew our paths would cross again and I'd have a chance to make amends, or at least try. A young man is too naïve to fix what he messes up, and an older man cares so much about mending what's broken it is all he can think about. There was no way I could ever forget. Fantasy, if you will let me, I'd like to keep in touch with you. I just want the opportunity to say and do what I should have so long ago. Forever! Victor

By the time Fantasy read the very last sentence she didn't know what to think. The one thing she wondered about had just happened. She opened the door and Victor had just walked through it.

Chapter 5

The daily grind had come to a peaceful, calm end. It was such a contrast to how his normally hectic days went. Today, there had been no one to reprimand for driving drunk. He didn't even have to speak to anyone about not following military protocol. Victor's day had not been filled with back-to-back meetings with hardly enough time for a break or lunch. His unhealthy eating habits and rushed lifestyle were the reasons he had come to depend on antacids and other remedies to soothe the discomfort he often had. There were so many reasons why life was out of sync for him, and he knew he had no one to blame but himself. Victor knew that he couldn't even fathom complaining when everything unfolded for him simply because of a little thing called karma. Nothing in any over-the-counter bottle or prescription written by a medical professional could provide the relief that he needed.

"What's good with you, Chief?" Darryl walked through the open door and plopped down in one of the chairs situated in front of Victor's large mahogany desk. Darryl Jones was one of the command chief master sergeants on base, and, aside from their work connection, the two were good friends. Their friendship spanned ten years, with this assignment being their third together. It wasn't often that there was a chance to really click, since faces changed often and friendships were not so easily established. But the two had become instant friends, and even when their tours took them in different directions, they talked often and their brotherly bond stayed that way.

"I'm good, man. An easy day, really. And, I tell you, I needed it." Victor picked up his pen, opened a folder, and signed a letter that needed to go out. The office Victor occupied at the Air Force base in Ramstein Germany was more like a deluxe suite and included a conference table with four chairs and two oversized built-in wall bookcases, both filled to capacity. There was a shelf the length of one of the walls that was used to display memorabilia and other trinkets from all over the world that were significant to his Air Force career, with a few of them holding only a personal value.

"That's good. My day was pretty breezy too." Darryl reached toward the desk, took the lid off the candy jar, and removed a peppermint.

"Every day is pretty breezy for you. Man, I swear, nothing ever gets to you." Victor looked at Darryl and how carefree he seemed as he popped the candy in his mouth. "I wish you'd give me some tips."

"You wouldn't listen if I did give you tips. In fact, bro, I've been tipping you for years and you always decide to take the worry road. I don't have time for all that. I just live it and forget it," Darryl said.

"Yeah, I know. But, as I said, today wasn't half bad, and not just because it wasn't a hectic day. There's another reason." Victor smiled slowly.

"Do tell." Darryl looked directly at his friend, not wanting to miss anything.

"I heard from an old friend yesterday." He tried to thumb through some papers and remain calm. In all honesty, hearing from Fantasy had him so excited, he had not thought of anything else since he read her message.

"Who'd you hear from?" Darryl was curious now. Victor never shared anything unless it was something that mattered to him.

"My college sweetheart," Victor said. "I hadn't heard from her since I left school to come into the Air Force."

"What's her name?" Darryl snapped his fingers while he tried to remember. "Let's see, it's a unique name, something from Disney."

Victor chuckled and decided to help Darryl out. "Fantasy."

"Yeah, that's it. How could I forget? You would always tell me she was the woman you should have married. Considering that the best thing about your marriage to Sonya is your daughter and my sweetie, Niya, Sonya's name should be the one I can't remember. Plus, man, you've never really talked about any other woman."

"I know." Victor rubbed his hand over his closely cut hair. "I just never thought I'd hear from her. Man, I was blown away."

"So, what happened? How did you hear from her?" Darryl quizzed. He was just as excited as his friend. He knew what hearing from her meant to Victor, and it couldn't have come at a better time. He and Sonya had been divorced for almost a year, and the remnant of the divorce saga was still carrying him through some major changes.

"You wouldn't believe it if I told you." Victor leaned forward, ready to spill his guts and share. He had been bursting all day to tell someone and since there was no one else to tell, Darryl would serve as his sounding board. His desk phone rang just as he was set to talk.

Victor put one finger up and answered, "Command Chief Charles." He spoke deeply into the receiver, much deeper than his usual voice. Somehow speaking real deep gave him a surge of power and authority, or maybe it was just all in his mind.

"Hello, Daddy." Niya's soft voice came through the phone line clearly.

Victor smiled. This just added to the good day he was having. "Hey gorgeous. How's my baby girl?"

Darryl returned the beaming look that Victor gave him. He was not a father yet, and since he had been waiting for the perfect ten, the ladies he met always came up short. He wasn't getting any younger, and because he wanted a son or daughter, he would have to downgrade his requirement to a perfect eight. His mother was a churchgoing woman, and he'd made it a point to request that she start calling out his need at the altar on Sunday morning and every time she joined her prayer partners. He went to the church on base, and to Bible Study every week along with Victor, but he knew that the more prayers that went up, the better his chances. Darryl wanted to believe that his lady love was on the expressway. He was waiting patiently with just a small amount of anxiety.

"I'm good. Hadn't talked to you since last week, and just as I was getting ready to Skype you yesterday, you signed off. I started to call and ask you to get back on but I figured you were tired and ready to go to bed."

"Oh, I'm sorry. I wasn't really tired. Bored maybe, but not tired. I wish you had called; I would have loved to see your smiling face."

Victor missed his daughter terribly. Niya joined Duke University as an honors student right after she spent a year abroad. Now, she was a senior with a dual major, and had been on the dean's list every semester. During the summer months and during breaks, they talked and Skyped every other day, but when school was in session, they committed to only once a week.

Niya was the apple of his eye and the most important person in his world. All the love and attention he'd lavished on her mother had gone unwanted and unwelcomed. When he finally accepted the truth of how she felt, he just added what Sonya didn't want to the abundance he already placed on their child.

"I know you would have, but you need to do you sometimes, Dad, I tell you that all the time and I don't think you really listen." Niya chuckled. Her dad was the best in her eyes. She would never desire that her parents stay together, since she'd grown up in a home that was one-sided: her dad giving all and her mother just receiving. Wise beyond her years, Niya had realized that long before her dad did. When Victor did realize it, he stayed anyway to ensure that she had a two-parent home. There were many times she wanted to tell him he didn't have to, but on the flip side of that he was her security blanket and she needed him to be there. Having only a part of him would have never been enough.

"I do listen. In fact, I'm getting ready to go eat some pizza and wings with Darryl." Victor knew what his daughter meant and he played it off. Talking about affairs of the heart and him moving on toward another woman didn't really feel that comfortable with the daughter of his ex-wife, the woman who had been his wife for twenty years.

"Oh, is Uncle Darryl there?"

"Yes. He is sitting across from me," Victor replied.

"Tell him hello," Niya said.

"Uncle Darryl, Niya says hello." Victor tilted the phone away from his mouth and spoke to Darryl.

"Tell baby girl hello," Darryl responded.

"You hear that?" Victor questioned Niya. He was pleased that his close friend had established an uncle-like kinship with his child.

"I did. But going out with Uncle Darryl is not what I meant. You are determined to make my job hard."

"And what is your job, little one?" he asked.

"To take care of you. You go on to dinner and we will Skype when you get home from work tomorrow. If that's okay with you?"

"I have no plans at all." Victor glanced over his schedule for the next day. It had already been printed out and placed on the corner of his desk. This was a common practice that had become a great time-managing habit. "I'll sign on the minute I get in and settle down."

"Okay, Daddy. Sounds like a plan," Niya said.

"Do you need anything?" He checked the calendar and noticed that her allotment should have already reached her checking account.

"Nope, my money hit the account a few days ago. Plus I went ahead and took the part-time job at The Gap."

"I told you, you didn't have to do that. You could have easily taken a class, or a few classes for that matter." Victor didn't want to deprive her of anything or any opportunity. Education was too important. He only wished that his parents could have afforded to pay for his education without him having to work part-time jobs just to stay in school. It got so overwhelming, since he wasn't the best academic student and he just got by.

"I am mentally drained and I need a break. I'm relaxing and enjoying hanging out with my friends, and the biggest perk is I get a discount. You know how I feel about clothes."

"I sure do." Victor laughed with her. "Well, baby girl, I'll talk with you tomorrow. Be good, safe, and I love you."

Darryl yelled, "I love you too."

"I love you both. Daddy, we will pick up where we left off."

"No problem." With that Victor hung up the phone. "Let's get out of here, Darryl."

The drive to the pizza joint took all of five minutes. Darryl pulled his Jaguar up next to Victor's BMW and got out. "Let's hit it, Chief. This big boy is hungry."

Darryl was a husky and pretty big guy, well over six foot two with 250 pounds of muscle. He was handsome and could turn more than a few heads. They say birds of a feather flock together, and he and Victor were together for much of their free time.

By the time they walked in and conversed with a few of their peers, more than an hour had passed since they had left the office.

"Hey, guys, you want a booth or a table?" The hostess moved in on them as soon as the guys walked away from them.

"We'll take whatever you have. I'm just ready to order and get some food in my belly." Darryl rubbed his stomach and glanced around the restaurant for an available space.

"No problem. I have a booth right over here. Just follow me." She was a strawberry blonde and had just the right cheery attitude to host people. She smiled and chit-chatted for the minute it took her to seat them, hand them menus, and tell them about the specials. "Jennifer will be with you in a minute. How about I bring you some breadsticks? Maybe that will tide you over." She looked over at Darryl and smiled, showing all her teeth.

"Cool. Thanks a lot," he said while opening the menu.

"I'm a little hungry myself, Chief," Victor said as he looked over the laminated pages of the menu. "I can't even recall what I had for lunch."

The hostess dropped off the breadsticks as promised. "Enjoy these while you wait."

Just as Darryl said thanks, their server came over. "Thanks, Heidi." She smiled, appreciating the assistance.

"No problem." Heidi gave Darryl a friendly wink.

The server said, "My name is Jennifer and I'll be serving you this evening. What can I get you two to drink?" She was dressed in a red polo shirt and black pants like the other workers, except her pants looked to be two sizes too small.

"I'll have iced tea, sweetened," Victor responded, and returned his focus to the menu.

"I'll have the same." Like Victor, Darryl was more concerned with the entrée than the drink. She could have easily brought him some water on the warm side without ice and it really wouldn't have mattered all that much.

"So, let's get back to our second reason for hanging out. How in the world did Fantasy find you?" Darryl closed his menu, satisfied with his dinner choice.

"Believe it or not, Facebook." Victor closed his menu too and looked at Darryl. "It seems that one of my fraternity brothers added her as a friend, and when she surfed around she saw me and thought she'd reach out."

"Dag. Who would have imagined. That social network stuff is no joke. I'm not up on it, but if it has brought back someone from your past, not to mention the love of your life, I'm going to join it right away."

"You should. I'm an advocate for life. I never thought I'd talk to her again." Victor leaned back against the booth and thought about it all again. It was still so fresh.

"So, tell me, what did she say? You are acting like she is willing to forgive you and hand over the keys to Fantasy Island or something." Darryl laughed out loud.

"That's the beauty of it all. She didn't say much. Just that she saw me and wanted to say hello. 'A blast from the past' is how she put it." A jazzy tune flowed through the restaurant, and Victor began to unwind and relax even more.

"Okay." Darryl rolled his hand, encouraging him to continue.

"Here you go." Heidi brought the drinks over. "Jennifer is handling two areas tonight and I'm helping her out. What are you guys having?"

"We'll make it easy. How about a large pizza with grilled chicken, Italian sausage, and extra cheese? And let us get an order of Buffalo wings with blue cheese." Darryl spoke without even breaking to breathe between items. He looked over at Victor. "Is that cool with you, Chief?"

"Works for me." Victor handed the menu back to the hostess.

"I'll get this right in for you." Once the order was taken, she turned and headed toward the kitchen.

"Well, my return message was a little longer than her message to me. And I sort of set the stage for all that I wanted to say. What's important right now is that I apologized." Victor looked around the restaurant and spotted a couple about their age. He watched as they held hands and looked deeply into each other's eyes. "I thought that was the most important thing to tell her. For years she likely thought I walked out because I was in love with Sonya, and that wasn't true. It was not the case at all."

"The story you told me sort of left your relationship with her up in the air. She thought you were breaking things off with Sonya for good, and before you could do that Sonya turns up pregnant. Fantasy cusses you flat out and you jet because you wanted to do the right thing and make your pops proud." Darryl recapped the story he had heard more than a few times over the years. That's what friends do. They listen when it is time to bare the soul and they do so without judging.

Victor listened, and, although it sounded a little callous, it was exactly how it had happened. "Yeah, that's how it all went down. I know I should have called, gone to visit her, or said something. But she said she never wanted to see me again. So, I went ahead and got married."

"You did what you thought was right." Darryl wondered if he would have done anything differently. Victor had been in a rough spot, and marriage, for an honorable guy who appeared to have it all together, was the logical thing to do.

"I did. But the thing is, Fantasy didn't think so. And from where she sat it didn't look like it. I was being honorable. It looked like I led her on and made her believe we were going to be together."

"That was then and years have passed. I'm sure if she still hated you, you would have never gotten a message from her."

"Yeah, I thought about that. But what if it's the opposite? Maybe she has come to seek some kind of revenge or to hire a hit." Victor sipped his iced tea and watched Darryl consume the breadsticks, as if inhaling them one by one. "In fact, I told her I looked outside, thinking she had sent someone after me."

"You didn't." Darryl wondered if that could be the truth. If they were in the States he would consider that a possibility, but being overseas he didn't think that she or any other woman would go to those lengths to get even.

"I did," said Victor. "In fact, I'm still looking over my shoulder."

"I'm sure she has gone on with her life. She sent you a message for old time's sake. I doubt you've been on her mind all this time." Darryl considered his next words, pondering what Fantasy would say next. "Wait until she sends you another message. By then you'll know what's on her mind, and how much more, if anything, you need to say, confess, or make amends for."

Victor thought about what Darryl was saying. He was the one who usually dripped with advice and wisdom. Tonight they had traded places. He needed to hear it though. The whole situation was that simple: Fantasy would accept his apology or she wouldn't. Either she would have contacted him with the hidden agenda of revenge and getting even at the top of her to-do list, or she would be the same caring individual he had gotten to know back then.

"You're right, man." Victor reflected on the evenings he used to watch Fantasy stroll through the lobby of Jacobs Hall while he worked the security desk. Most of the time she was in the company of a few of her friends, and other times she was alone. Even in the solitude of her own company it never seemed that she wasn't comfortable or totally at ease.

There was something different about her. He knew that even before they'd had their first real conversation. Before then, they had only shared a quick hello and a slight grin. Still Victor could see it. Fantasy was not like some of the others. She seemed to know what she wanted, and while she tried to seem like she'd do anything to get it, Victor saw through that. She boasted that she hailed from the tough streets of Brooklyn, and when she hung out with the sisterhood she bragged about living for the moment and doing things that were on the edge. Being one of the big brothers of her sisterhood group, he watched in quiet observation; however, he felt that what she shared was what she wanted others to think. It wasn't even close to who she really was. For some reason unbeknownst to him at that time, she wanted desperately to fit in, to belong. She sheltered her feelings and didn't let anyone in.

One day after confiding in Fantasy and venting because of the crazy changes Sonya was putting him through, she let her defenses down and they quickly became friends. It wasn't long before he won his way into her life and into her heart. The problem was that, in the end, Victor knew he wrecked her life and proved not to be the person she thought he was.

He knew it hurt Fantasy deeply when he went back to Sonya after the two of them had crossed the line and ended up sleeping together. Victor had fallen in love with Fantasy, and sleeping with her, even though they had planned to wait, had happened because neither of them could control the inferno that was ignited when they were in the same room. He knew that Fantasy felt played, and she never gave him a chance to explain.

Victor knew that if she was ever going to forgive him now, he would have to somehow make her see that playing her was never a part of his plan. What they shared was never a game. It meant everything to him, and hindsight was telling him it still did.

Chapter 6

"Fantasy, I swear, all we do lately is pig out." Nick picked up a rib covered with sauce and took a huge bite. He licked his lips and talked through the mouthful. "I came over here just to drop off the research. You could have at least warned me that you had picked up the entire takeout menu from Mert's. All this binge eating is not for me. I know I'm your best friend, but I'm not commiserating with whatever it is you are going through with food. I'll do anything else, but this sort of makes me feel a little funny. A little girly."

Fantasy giggled. She had to admit that she did have Nick agreeing to some things that could appear to be a little on the feminine side. "Nick, I'm sorry. I know that you are all man, and not because I've slept with you, but because I know you and what you like." She reached over the chicken, hot links, and ribs, picked up the container of potato salad and plopped some on her plate.

"I mean, last week we were curled up on the sofa watching *Waiting to Exhale* and eating Godiva chocolate cheesecake. I went to the mall with you to pick out some intimate apparel. Dag, girl, I'm trying to stay in touch with my mack. We'll have to marry each other because no one else will want us."

"What you talking about, Nick? We are hot commodities. Dee is sweating you daily, and if I were interested

I'm sure I could enter the dating game," she stated flatly, and stabbed a hot link with her fork.

"Okay. I'm going to ask you to step away from the food. You are overdosing on soul food. Sweetie, you don't even normally eat this much." He rubbed her arm as she placed a forkful of baked beans into her mouth.

"I know; I don't know what's up with me. This has been going on for a few weeks and I can't make any sense of my actions, reactions, or anything. Maybe it's some type of hormonal imbalance."

"Okay, I'm not listening." Nick covered his ears and started to sing. "La, la, la. La, la, la."

"Nick, stop acting silly. Seriously, I don't know. I plan to check it out when I return from Chicago. Right now, there's something else I want to tell you."

"As long as it doesn't include talk of your sexual escapades or what you're doing to substitute for what's missing." He leaned back against the cushion of the sofa, too full to eat another bite. He was making light of it all, but he was a little worried about Fantasy. Nick knew that she hadn't been feeling her best. Then there was this emotional rollercoaster. It was just so unlike her. It went without saying that he'd do whatever he could to figure out what was going on.

"Well, it has nothing to do with the present, but everything to do with the past," Fantasy said.

"Okay, I'm listening."

"I took Kam's advice and created a Facebook account," Fantasy started. She crossed her legs and rocked her left bare foot back and forth. She was dressed casually in a pair of jeans and an orange fitted tank.

"I knew that. We talked about it right after you created your profile, remember?"

"Yes, I remember sharing that with you." Fantasy sighed. "There's more. I was surfing around the other night on the page of an old college friend and I stumbled upon Victor." She looked around the room as if someone other than Nick had heard her revelation.

"Victor Charles?" Nick questioned. This was not their first conversation about Victor Charles, but it had been years since she had even brought him up. The first time had been a year after he and Fantasy became friends.

"Yes, that Victor. Anyway, I went back and forth and before I knew it I'd sent him a message." Fantasy stood up, walked over to the fireplace mantle, and rubbed her fingers over the framed graduation photo of Kam. The day he'd taken the photo was only one of the many happy moments in her life. He had brought her so much joy and happiness. "I wanted to see if he was going to respond." She turned back around. "I just wanted to know what he would say to me after all this time." She went back over to where Nick reclined, and positioned herself in the oversized side chair. Fantasy folded her hands in her lap and tried to pull herself away from the light. She wasn't Carol Anne, but she knew somebody should be warning her to walk away from the light.

Nick said nothing, but focused his full attention on what she was saying. His sense of humor wasn't needed; what was needed was a listening ear. He knew that Victor surfacing was a throwback that had to have Fantasy's mind reeling. Sure, she'd told him on more than one occasion that it was over and that ship had sailed. She had even gone so far as to thank God for delivering her from that situation and allowing her to get over the love. He went to church right alongside her and gave praise with her, but every now and then there was something in her eyes that kept the memory of Victor alive. He just never wanted to tell her he still saw it.

"Nick, after all this time . . . It was a déjà vu moment. I feel like I opened up a Pandora's box, and good common sense is saying to close the darn thing up."

"Well, what did he say?" He was trying to wait for her to get to that point. It was taking her a minute and he needed to know.

"That he had thought of me throughout the years. He confessed that he was naïve and dumb, and that things had ended badly. He apologized, and what was shocking was that the entire premise of the message sounded like he expected me to forgive him. He even said something about keeping in touch." Fantasy threw her hands up in the air in mental defeat.

"Fantasy, you had to expect him to say all that. I mean, if that's been on his mind all these years, he was likely relieved to finally be able to say those two little words." He eyed her and watched her left eyebrow arch. "I'm just saying, Fantasy. I'm a man and we do some stupid stuff, but once the smoke settles and reality kicks our butt, we have a need to want to make things right."

"Nick, what he did was hurtful. I mean, going back to Sonya was one thing, but me finding out that they were getting married from everyone else but him . . ." She sat back. "It may not have felt any better coming from him, but it definitely tore me apart hearing it from our circle. There was no way I wouldn't have found out. Victor knew that."

"Fantasy, he probably didn't know how to tell you." Nick received the same raised eyebrow from his friend. He had to take the hard looks if he was going to help her find a level of sanity where at least some of what had happened would make sense, and, even more, a level where what was happening between the two was rational.

"I crept around in secret, meeting him off campus in the wee hours of the morning like some no-class, low-budget hussy. All because he needed time to dissolve things with Sonya. But there was the promise that he was going to end things with her, and that was what I held on to. It just never happened, and I don't think he ever intended for it to end." She fell deeper into the pit of what had occurred between them. "I listened to him talk about her. Even though I knew she was a trifling nobody, I never badmouthed her. And what did I get? He didn't even have the decency to tell me personally that he was going to marry her."

"I get it." Nick didn't know what to say. He didn't know how to console his friend. This pain was preexisting and it had lasted twenty-one years; what could he say to that? How could he help her fix it? She was supposed to be delivered from it and was a better person because she experienced the heartbreak. All of what she expressed was a mirage. He had known it then, and it was especially true now. He moved from the sofa to the ebony table centered on the ultra-modern printed rug. Nick reached over, and Fantasy fell into his arms and cried silently.

Neither of them spoke for more than thirty minutes. The silence and the heaviness that loomed over them said it all. She was still hurting. It was a door she'd opened with no clue that she would come face-to-face with something that she had not resolved. He felt her ache with every labored breath she took.

Finally, when no more tears would come and Fantasy knew she had made a complete fool of herself, she moved away from Nick and wiped her eyes with her fingertips. He was her best friend and she could be real.

But even with Nick she always held it together. She was always strong. There was never a sign of weakness that anyone could see when they looked at her. It had been that way when she stood stone-faced in front of her mother's dead body. It remained when they lowered Valerie in the ground that cold, cold winter day. That chill in her soul stayed; it had remained until Victor.

"I'm good. In fact, I'm better than good, and I know exactly what I will say to Command Chief Master Sergeant Victor Charles." Fantasy wiped the rest of the tears away.

"I'm glad you are cool." Victor looked at her cock-eyed. He even slid back a little, just in case this was the cool before she blew and her temper erupted like a volcano. "Fantasy, baby, honey. What do you have planned? And, keep in mind, I don't look good in a jumpsuit, and while I like being restrained, it's for entertainment purposes only."

Fantasy laughed through the residue of pain. "I know; you are such a freak."

"And game recognizes game." Nick joined her laughter.

"Well, after all this time, maybe finding Victor is a stroke of luck. It would be a shame not to give him the opportunity to make amends. And it would be a shame this time around not to turn the tables."

"What are you saying?" Nick quizzed, although he had an idea where she was going with this.

"Two can play. And since he is one up, it's my turn." She laughed heartily and, after a second, it sounded a little wicked.

Nick watched wide-eyed and prayed that her head didn't start spinning. Love could make you do some crazy things and it could carry you to a place you would never dare go on your own. He continued to look at Fantasy, and knew she was already at that place.

Chapter 7

The rush of the week had Fantasy moving faster than she wanted to. She'd had no clue when she boarded the express flight to Chicago that this assignment would have so many layers. It was originally planned that she would interview Monica Kinkaid, the lady who was dismissed from her upper-management position at a leading car company because she refused to change her hairstyle. She had decided to start growing dreadlocks a few years ago. While they were short, and looked like what could be passed off as a short twist hairstyle, they had been acceptable, but once they hit her shoulders and took on a trendy life of their own, she was called in and asked to make a change, or else.

This was a story her news director wanted her to do. There were a few other people available but he decided that Jordan would do the best job. She wanted to be offended, but the other writers were white and she was, of course, of color.

Fantasy, aka Jordan Alexander, didn't argue the point, because it was actually a story she was interested in doing. Sure, she was in touch with her inner beauty and didn't see anything wrong with other women, or men for that matter, expressing themselves through their hairstyles, but she was still holding to her salon-straight hair with no desire to go nappy. Power to Ms. Monica, she figured, for her liberated hair style.

"Hey, Nana." Fantasy walked through the lobby of the elegant Sutton Place Hotel and glanced up at the glass ceiling that reflected a glitter of sparkling light everywhere she looked. It was already Friday and she hadn't had a chance to reach out and touch anybody.

"Hello, Fantasy. I've been waiting for you to call. I even told your grandfather that we would likely get a call today. You never go the entire length of your trip without calling us," Pearl said to her granddaughter, more relieved than she knew.

"You know I would call. I've just been so busy. It's been a whirlwind from the time I stepped off the plane. I had no idea this assignment would be this involved."

"You can handle it. There's no doubt in my mind that you can. Sometimes things get a little difficult. Just dig deep. Nothing worthwhile comes without hard work."

Fantasy thought about what her grandmother was saying. All that she had accomplished was afforded by the hard work she had put in for years and her continuous effort to stay at the top of her career. She'd jumpstarted her goals by using a little of the money she inherited from her mother to buy the house and to educate her son. Even then, there were mixed feelings about how it came to be and what she gave up to have what her mother called, "more than enough wealth." Fantasy went above and beyond trying to erase the memories of her not-so-pleasant growing-up years and, over time, success became an adrenaline rush.

It was decided early in her career that Fantasy Delight Whitman wasn't exactly a suitable name in the worlds of journalism. She adopted the professional name Jordan Alexander and became well known in all the right circles. She was at the top of her profession. Valerie Whitman may have had other ideas for what her baby girl would become, but her daughter's future included the wonderful world of media. That was a far cry from being a chip off her mother's block. No, Fantasy Delight Whitman, aka Jordan Alexander, ended up as a journalist for one of the largest news syndicates: an ultimate gig that provided enough revenue to cover all of her needs and plenty of her wants. Plus, it provided a lavish existence for her best half, Kameron.

Fantasy used her card key to gain access to the presidential suite. This was just one of the many company perks. They made sure that she was comfortable wherever they sent her to complete an assignment. She guessed they were trying to make sure she had some of the comforts of home.

"I know. I just get a little frustrated sometimes. I just don't want to lose sight of what is important." She wasn't sure why she just said what she'd said; working hard at her profession had always been important. Until lately.

She removed her peep-toed black pumps and walked farther into the suite. Fantasy was dressed in simple black slacks and a sheer overlay periwinkle blue wide-arm blouse with a black silk cami underneath. It was extremely hot outside, and she had pulled her hair back in a side twist and secured it with several pins and a black hair clip with rhinestones. A few curls fell loosely on both sides. For jewelry she wore pearl studs, and an illusion chain with a single suspended pearl teardrop that nestled itself between her ample bosom.

"I'm sure you will do well. You always do." Pearl took a seat at the kitchen table and wiped it with the towel she was holding, even though there wasn't anything to wipe. "You make me so proud."

Fantasy blushed as she sat down on the loveseat. "I know, and I never grow bored of hearing you tell me so. Did Kam call?"

"He did. He phoned the day you left. Let's see, what was that, Wednesday?" Pearl thought for a moment. "Yeah, it was Wednesday night. He talked to me and Matthew. I think they talked about that fishing trip. Kam will be coming home to go. Matthew is so excited that Kam is going along. That's all he's talked about for days."

"Yeah, he told me he and Granddad were planning a man's man weekend. Like we don't want to go fishing." Fantasy knew she didn't. She knew her Nana didn't either.

"Child, you know neither of us wants anything to do with hooking or catching no fish. Now, I'm one up on you because I can clean and cook them. You can only cook them, and that's occasionally." She grinned, thinking about the sight Fantasy made the first time she attempted to clean fish. She couldn't even stand to touch the skin of the fish.

"All right. You got me. Is this the same fishing trip in South Carolina that the men of the church go on every summer?"

"Yes, they go every year. He goes because it's an annual thing. Truthfully, he don't care nothing about going with them old windbags, talking about what they used to do and lying about what they think they can still do. Girl, them old Viagra-taking men are a mess."

"Please don't tell me my grandfather is taking Viagra. That's more information than I need." Fantasy put her hand up. She didn't even want to think about her grandparents still getting it on.

"I won't say then. What I will say is that he keeps a smile on my face." Pearl Whitman giggled like a young girl talking about her first sexual escapade.

"Nana, I'm done." Fantasy laughed with her grandmother. "Listen, I have one last meeting, which includes dinner, so I have just enough time for a nap and to shower."

"Okay, sweetie. Call me the minute you get back home."

"I will. Love you. Kiss Granddad for me."

"I will. Have a safe flight, and I'll be praying for you," Pearl added.

"I know. Talk to you tomorrow." She lightly touched the end button on the cell phone.

Fantasy reached for the remote and turned on the television. Not wanting to take a nap with news of current events in the background, she stopped at a rerun episode of Sanford and Son. She hadn't seen the show in forever. She curled up and relaxed against the cushion of the sofa and watched the familiar episode. She laughed at all the funny parts as if this were her first time watching it.

Looking down at her phone, she decided to check her e-mail on it to avoid walking over to the desk and waking up her computer. There wasn't really anything to check on from her office. Her assistant had updated her a few hours ago. Really, she was wondering if Victor had sent another message. There had been a total of six messages since he responded to the initial one she had sent. Fantasy had wanted to respond to each and every one, but, remembering the rules of the game, she knew she should be slow in responding, as if too busy to do so. She wanted him to think that, and she wanted to show that responding was not a priority. In other words, she was playing hard to get. It must have been working, because when she checked out her Facebook account last night his last line was a plea to please get back to him.

Since the first response, she had also learned that he was overseas, stationed in Germany. A few of the messages came in the early hours of the morning, when he should have been asleep. Additionally, he had added his e-mail address, and office and house phone. Victor had given her every possible method to reach him. While he hadn't really disclosed much about his personal life, his promise in one message was that he would share everything with her. The one thing he did make known was that he was no longer married to Sonya.

Deciding it was time to answer his messages, Fantasy opened the application on her cell phone, but then decided against that. She walked over to the desk and pulled the chair out. She tapped a key, and, while she waited for the laptop to come to life, she removed her sheer blouse. Fantasy stood up and opened the curtain slightly to allow a little more light to stream through the window. It was 3:00, and she looked below as people moved along the busy street. It was such a spectacular view from up where she was. Moving gingerly back to the chair, she rubbed her knee. The pain had nagged her worse than ever over the past few weeks. She'd take something before her nap.

Once she opened the Facebook account, she went directly to her messages, expecting to see just the message from early this morning. But it seemed that Victor had left a message less than ten minutes ago. That made her smile. Fantasy spoke out loud. "You are after me. Let's see, what do I say?"

Fantasy read his message, which mentioned how busy he had been. He also said he was waiting for her response, and that he hoped she hadn't regretted contacting him. It ended with another plea and his sincere desire to right the wrong. There was no way, in her opinion, that the wrong could be righted. The ball was in her court and she would determine how the game would be played.

Hello, Victor. Sorry for my delay in responding. I've been extremely busy. In fact, I'm out of town for work. I was so pleased that you took the time to respond. Honestly, I believed that you had forgotten me, although I had not forgotten you. There is so much catching up we need to do and I'm looking forward to it. There is no need for continued apologies; we were both young then and life has unfolded well for both of us. Let's let bygones be bygones. I'll return home on Saturday, and once I'm settled I'll contact you with a possible time that we can chat by phone. Until then, Fantasy

She smiled to herself right after she hit send. Something stirred in her that was tied to her sense of rightness. But she was focused on creating a false illusion for Victor. She would fake that her sole purpose in contacting him was to become friends again. After he was hooked with that, she would say she still remembered what they shared, and then she'd tell him that she was still in love with him. At that point, her plan was to open up and allow him to fall madly in love with her. Once they entered the head-over-heels part, she'd end things and shut off all communication with him. For that reason, she would share as little of her life as possible and stay disengaged. It wouldn't be easy to accomplish her goal; however, it would be necessary.

Turning off the computer, Fantasy finished undressing and slipped on a Victoria's Secret nightshirt. She set her cell phone to ring at 6:00 and called the desk to arrange a backup call at 6:15. Derrick Stedman, the CEO of the company, would be meeting her in the hotel restaurant at 7:30. This would tie the entire assignment up with a bow, and at the conclusion she would be able to put everything together and have it all ready to run by next week.

She pulled the lightweight cover and sheet back and slipped inside the bed. There was another episode of Sanford and Son coming on and her plan was to watch it in its entirety, believing that sleep would not come quickly. Her thoughts reflected on the first night she spent with Victor. Fantasy turned on her back and closed her eyes, and it began.

"So tell me, Fantasy, when are you going to let me take you out?" Carl questioned, looking at her with a hound-like look on his face. He was a cute guy and just as popular as the other members of his clique. She just never fell all over him like just about every other female in their circle.

"No time. I don't do one-nighters, and, from what I hear, that's all you do," Fantasy replied, and sucked her teeth.

"You heard wrong. I'm a good guy. It's the brotherhood that catches a bad rap. I'm probably one of the best guys in the fraternity." Carl was pleading his case.

"Hold up, frat. You act as if I'm not sitting here. I know you're not going to put me down with the rest of them," Victor interjected, not at all pissed but just clearing up what his friend had said.

"Victor, you know you're my boy. And you're one of the good guys, but need I remind you that you are off the market, bro? Sonya got you on lock, so you are not capable of playing."

Fantasy looked directly at Victor and narrowed her eyes in disbelief. Their initial icebreaker had been their walk a month ago. That's when he'd confessed that he liked her. Since that first time, they had hung out off campus numerous times. Victor had also shared that he was breaking it off with Sonya. Now, here was his boy, Carl, informing her that it hadn't happened.

"I don't believe any of you guys. I'm sorry to say I'm connected in any way. From this point on I'm going to do my best to separate myself. Victor, I expected more from you." She stood and walked away, knowing that he was fully aware of what she was saying.

"Fantasy, you know me better than that." Victor's eyes were saying more than his words were sharing. "Don't let this boy fill your head."

"Whatever. I'm going to bed." Fantasy left them both there.

Two hours later she heard a light knock on her door. She was barely asleep, but she knew it could only be Victor. She opened the door and there he was.

The first thing he did was apologize for what Carl had said. "Hey." Victor closed the door behind him, not wanting to be seen. "I had to come up and tell you that Carl was just tripping."

"Really?" Fantasy folded her arms across her chest, partly because she was upset and partly because she was trying to cover her chest. She wore a sleeveless ruffled-bottom baby-doll gown with matching panties. It was a Friday night, and since she was going to wash her hair the next day she hadn't bothered to tie it up or roll it. It hung loosely around her head, and she was hoping that it looked presentable at that moment, since she hadn't even taken the time to check it out in the nearby mirror.

"Sonya and I have been at it. I mean, she's been going off on me and I'm telling her every day that it's not working, that we aren't going to work. It would have ended by now, but she was talking some crazy suicide stuff and I just didn't want to hear it. So, I've just been keeping my distance."

"So you really think Sonya is going to kill herself if you break up with her?" Fantasy asked him.

"You don't know Sonya like I do. She's capable of anything. But I'm going to tell her soon. I have to. Fantasy, I love you."

Before Fantasy had a chance to say anything else, Victor came close and kissed her lips softly.

"I could get lost in your kisses." Victor stood in the center of the room, holding her tightly. Before he said anything else, he claimed her lips again. This time the kiss was deeper than before.

The room was dim, and only the light from the corner shined through the curtained window. Her roommate had gone home for the weekend. Victor had known that Fantasy was alone from a conversation he'd heard her having earlier with one of her friends she was signing in. When he'd gotten off duty, he made his way to her door and hoped that she would let him in. He wanted to just look at her. Just be in her presence.

He had kissed her before, but it had never been like this. It was never that soft; his mouth had never been that warm. When he pulled away all she could do was look up at him.

Victor never took his eyes off her, but moved with her toward her bed.

Before she knew it, the backs of her legs hit the bed and she fell back. Still, their eyes continued to be locked on one another, and he fell lightly on top of her.

They kissed until neither of them could breathe. The entire room seemed to spin on some axis that Fantasy could not even explain. Her head was spinning along with the room and everything from her neck down was ablaze. At intervals Victor paused and told her how good she felt and how very much he loved her. He even promised that they would be together forever. He said he wanted her to be his wife. He wanted her to go with him after his basic training.

She fell more in love with him as he shared so much with her. She believed every word, so when it came time for the next logical step in their relationship, Fantasy knew she was ready.

"I want you." Victor could hardly get the words out. His rock-hard anatomy was pressing against her thigh.

She felt it and knew even without looking or touching that it was big. She had to tell him that she was a virgin and that all her talk about being experienced had not been true.

"Victor, I want you, but there is something I need to tell you." Fantasy swallowed, not wanting to turn him off or have him think she was a tease.

Victor slowly placed one finger over her lips and then kissed her softly again. He opened her mouth with his tongue and didn't stop until their tongues mated. "I already know, and I love you. I want the gift you are offering and I promise I won't hurt you."

She relaxed and allowed him to take full control. He continued to kiss her and caress her. She wasn't even sure she remembered when his clothes hit the floor, but right after he removed her gown and the panties, they were both under the sheets. Again, he promised not to hurt her, and once he moved on top of her and shifted his weight so as not to be too heavy, he looked down into her eyes. Fantasy held on to him for dear life, and while she looked up into his gentle eyes, it happened. Her mouth opened wide as she felt the sudden pain that lasted for a few minutes, and then the pain left and the pleasure began.

It went on for hours, but each moment was more intense and more passionate than the moment before. She didn't know love between two people could be like this. She didn't know it could feel so good.

From the cracked doors of the house her mother ran she had watched sex happen in the rooms and it never looked like this. The sounds and words held no romance, and the ladies who were like family to her never held on to the men who were in bed with them. It was, as they told her, work.

What she felt for Victor at that moment was special, and she wanted to hold on to him and never let him go. The thought of protection had not been discussed, and, after it was all over, she realized that he had not used anything either. The chance of getting pregnant in her young mind was impossible the first time around. And so what? Victor loved her and she loved him. What could possibly go wrong?

Snapping out of the memory, Fantasy opened her eyes and her heart ached. She wasn't sure what ached more: her heart or her body. She had remembered every moment of that first time. Her reflection down memory lane just acknowledged that it was still intact; his words, all of his promises. She thought of that night and the wonderful cloud she had been on during the days that followed. She remembered the heartbreak when the promise was broken.

There was another reason why that first night was so vivid in her mind. It was the night that Kameron had been conceived.

Chapter 8

"Thank you, Doc. I'm sure it's nothing. I've just been having a few aches and pains here and there. I finally decided not to ignore it any longer, but to come on over and have it checked out." Victor was sitting on the examination table, going over his symptoms with one of the doctors on staff at the base's medical facility.

"I'm sure everything is fine, Chief. But, in the meantime, I'm going to give you something a little stronger for the acid reflux. The nausea really shouldn't be a daily occurrence. But the acid reflux itself is a pretty common illness for someone in a high-ranking position like you. I guess you can say a certain amount of stress comes with the territory." The balding doctor wrote on his prescription pad.

"Don't I know it," Victor spoke up. "This assignment has been a blessing, but it has not been without its challenges. I'm reminded, though, that success often comes at a cost."

"Yes, but that cost shouldn't be your health. You must learn to work smart. That's the key to longevity. Learning to work smart does not include the description you gave me of your typical day." He ripped the paper he wrote on from his pad. "I'm also going to give you something to help you rest. Now, don't fuss, but take it when you have had an extremely long day, or if you've had a stressful day. It will, hopefully, help your body balance."

"I don't think I'll be taking that, but go ahead and write the prescription." Victor didn't want to tell the doctor that what he needed to relieve his stress was not at the pharmacy. There was one way he loved to enjoy relieving his stress and it included a woman he could call his own. Now that he had no wife and no one in the wings waiting to be Mrs. Charles, there was a measure of physical frustration. He was praying more and hoping that one day things would change.

"Also, Chief, I'd like to order a few tests. Again, nothing to worry about. I'm just concerned about your lack of energy, your sleeping habits, the nausea, and the dizziness. I'll write an order for what I'd like them to do and you can go over tomorrow to get it all taken care of."

"I have a few morning meetings." Victor began to mentally go over his calendar for the next day. After the doctor recapped all the symptoms that he had shared, he was a little more concerned than before. It hadn't seemed like he was dealing with so much, since the symptoms rarely bothered him at the same time.

"It's an order." The doctor smiled. He didn't want to sound alarmed. Years of practice and patient observation were alerting him that a few things were not adding up, and he wanted to be able to dismiss his theory.

"I guess I can arrange to miss the meetings." Victor stood up. "Thanks for squeezing me in."

"No problem at all. Make sure you get these filled right away." The doctor stood up and extended his hand. "It's good meeting you, Chief Charles."

"You too, sir. Have a great day." Victor left the examination room. As he walked out of the facility, he exchanged smiles and pleasant nods until he was outside the medical office. His job to be all smiles and jovial wasn't always easy. His position and status on the base called for him to be just that. It sort of went along with the stripes and bars he wore.

Once he walked outside he looked around. It was a better-than-average day. Usually the temperature was on the cool side, but it was actually warm today. The sun felt good against his face as he lifted up his head. He thought about the message he'd received from Fantasy on Friday night. He had quickly replied, but didn't expect a message back soon since she had mentioned that she would be getting into town late Saturday night. Still, her message made him smile. In a nutshell, she had shared that she was willing to listen to him. They would be arranging a time to talk on the phone and he was looking forward to it. It may have seemed like a small accomplishment to some, but this had been years in the making and he couldn't wait. He almost wanted to go out and buy a new pair of jeans to wear for the occasion, but it was a call and she would not be seeing him. Victor laughed to himself. This woman already had him gone. What he was sure she didn't know was that he was still in love with her. He had always loved her, and as the years had gone by he was so aware of the love he still harbored.

He gave Sonya so much and went to great lengths, and yet he was never able to give himself completely. Out of loyalty and his personal commitment to his marriage and his daughter, he would have never taken an out. He would have stayed miserable and unhappy: a small price to honor his vows. But her cheating and lack of commitment came to an ugly head. He was forced out, and once he was safely on the other side, safely in the divorce zone, life was already orchestrating the next phase. While there had seemed to be nothing in store for him, no silver lining in sight, out of the blue, along came Fantasy. It had to be a sign that things were going to get better.

Once Victor got in his car, he removed his cell phone from the holder on his waist. He called the office and waited for his assistant, Marie Lopez, to pick up. "Good morning, this is Chief Charles. Do I have any messages?"

"No. Everything is quiet on the work front," Lopez answered.

"I checked my BlackBerry, and, according to what I see here, I don't have any meetings for the rest of the day. Is that correct?" Victor was direct, and hoped that she would spend extra minutes recapping what he already knew.

"Affirmative, sir. Your afternoon is all clear," Lopez responded.

"Well, I'm going to do something I rarely do. I'm taking the rest of the day off." Victor wasn't exactly sure when he had decided to take the day off. He wasn't feeling up to par and maybe a day of rest would do him good. He'd hit the assignment floor running and had been at one speed since he'd walked into his office. Unfortunately, from what the doctor said, that speed had been high. Truthfully, he may have burned himself out. He came straight from a hectic assignment in northern Virginia, ended his marriage, and relocated overseas all in the span of one year.

"Sir, are you okay?" Lopez asked out of concern. "I know you had a medical appointment." She respected Chief Charles a lot and thought he was a great boss. She knew a lot about him both professionally and personally. After all, Lopez had been his assistant since his arrival there. What he didn't know was that she was attracted to him. The problem was that she knew better than to cross the line just like that. He lived in a glass house and she didn't even want to chance sneaking around to see him. Not that he would. From the time he'd assumed his post he had shown no interest toward any woman. No one called his office other than his daughter and, on a few occasions, his ex-wife. The calls from the ex ended almost before they began. Lopez knew because she had timed each call he received from her.

As far as she could tell, and from the way he carried himself, she didn't peg him to be a down-low brother. She assumed that he was just driven and focused on his job and career. There was nothing wrong with that, but he had to be lonely. Maybe one day, if there was an opening for such a conversation, she would quiz him and, who knew; if there was a will, there had to be a way. He was a beautiful brown specimen of a man and sexy didn't begin to describe him. Marie was willing to take whatever he offered, figuring Chief Charles was worth the wait.

Every day she made sure she was at her desk ten minutes early just to inhale his fragrance as he walked by her desk. He would often linger over her desk to ask a question or review something, giving her a chance to relish in the nearness of him. She knew she had to take it slow and make her moves cautiously if she was to be the next woman in his bed.

Marie couldn't help but fantasize about a life with him. She would have no problem leaving her struggling life behind and living in the wealth that he could afford her. She was confident that once he sampled what she had to offer he would be hooked, and the rest would be history.

"I'm fine. Just planning to do a little work from home and rest. I'll see you in the morning. If something comes up, feel free to call me. Have a good day." Victor clicked off his phone. He thought about calling Darryl to see if his schedule was open long enough to hang out and play a little racquetball. Then again, he remembered that his purpose for being off was to relax.

With that mental reminder, Victor decided that he would pick up the prescriptions, grab a few things from the grocery store, and go directly to his apartment. It wasn't exactly the brightest spot in his life, and it was far from home in décor and feel, but he made the best of it.

Living in a lavish 5,200-square-foot space could really spoil anyone. Victor had spent so much time picking out and purchasing a home in the last two places they had lived. From the onset, his primary goal had not been to just pick out a house with certain amenities, but he was focused on creating a home for them. With little help from Sonya he had decorated both homes and was proud of all he had done. There was a little sadness in leaving their home in Ohio, but once they settled in northern Virginia, the new residence they'd purchased screamed home in no time. Even though Niya was away at Duke more than she was at home, she added her touches to their northern Virginia residence. It wasn't long before the two felt at home, although Sonya remained slightly detached from the house and from them.

Victor wanted to believe that it was a phase, something she'd go through and return to a better state of mind from. Maybe she would be even better than in the beginning. The truth was that she never did come back. His wife, the mother of his child, was more comfortable in the arms of the man she had seen off and on for all the years they had been married. At least he could say it had not been several men, a point Sonya had boasted about, as if you could boast about any form of infidelity. It didn't matter that Victor had only competed with one man for his wife's affection. In the end he had lost and the other guy won.

Victor put all the groceries away and changed, putting on a pair of gym shorts and a T-shirt. He elected to do some cleaning and laundry while cooking a filling and healthy meal. On a daily basis he lived off of frozen meals and takeout. Occasionally, he would eat with Darryl or some of the young airmen. Of course, there were the almost weekly events that so often included appetizers and dinner. In short, even in the company of other people, he was tired of eating alone, because he wasn't enjoying the company of someone he cared to share dinner conversation with and someone who honestly cared about how his day went.

The soothing sound of jazz flowed through the apartment while he waited for pork chops to grill. In keeping with the balanced meal concept, he prepared and placed a potato in the oven to bake, steamed broccoli, and tossed a small salad.

He checked the chops and the potato one last time, and gauged that in another ten minutes his home-cooked meal would be ready to enjoy. His stomach growled at the thought and the wonderful aroma that filled the entire place.

The computer was situated on a nearby desk, and, while he had been determined to cook first and handle some chores, he had done just that and was ready for a few minutes' break. By the time he logged in and checked his e-mail, Fantasy had just left a message.

Victor couldn't help but smile as he read and reread the e-mail. She wanted him to call her at noon her time. That would be 6:00 his time. Victor glanced down at the time on his computer and noticed that he had about three more hours before he needed to make the most important call of his life. He'd be on pins and needles until the clock displayed that precise time. "What can I do until then?" he questioned himself out loud.

Victor went into the kitchen to finish cooking his meal. He was on a cloud knowing that in a few short hours he would be talking with Fantasy again after all these years. Sending e-mails and messages back and forth was one thing, but tonight he would hear her voice.

He listened and hummed to the music as he placed his dinner on one of his nicer plates, poured a big glass of tea, and sat down at the table. He forced himself to eat even though he had no appetite and was full of nervous energy. He could never tell Fantasy—or Darryl, for that matter—how nervous he felt at the anticipation of talking to her again. He would lose too many cool points with Darryl, and Fantasy would likely think he was whipped. He was; he just wasn't ready for her to know that yet.

What he could taste of the meal he'd prepared wasn't half bad. He immediately did the dishes and cleaned everything up. The rest of his energy was spent folding clothes and cleaning the bathroom. By the time he did all that he was a little winded, which didn't make a lot of sense. He decided he wouldn't borrow trouble, meaning he wouldn't get all worked up trying to figure out what was going on. Before opening the worry door, which he was determined to keep closed, or taking on anything else that he really wasn't up for, Victor sat down in his catnap recliner and decided to watch a movie. That was his favorite pastime. Time was a commodity he had plenty of. Living single in a small apartment far away from home and having so much time on his hands made it easy to become the king of movies. He picked up the latest ones he saw at the store, ordered them online, and kept up with whatever else was coming out. The German channels didn't offer a lot of American shows or a variety of anything, so that left movies as a great alternative for staying entertained.

Victor loaded a DVD into the player and sat back in the recliner across from the flat-screen television. In no time at all, he was totally relaxed. He checked the time and noticed that he still had an hour before he needed to make the call.

Shortly after the movie started, exhaustion hit him without warning. His eyes got a little heavy, and he decided there would be no harm in taking a power nap. It was a major mistake; when Victor opened his eyes it was 7:30. He wanted to kick himself. The last thing he needed was for Fantasy to think that he wasn't going to call at all or didn't care enough to be on time. Either way, it wasn't a good way to start their first conversation. Without even checking to see if she had sent a message asking what had happened, he dialed frantically.

"Hello," Fantasy spoke into the phone. She had been waiting for Victor's call, and when she had waited more than an hour, she decided to get some work done. She almost greeted the caller by saying "Jordan Alexander," because she had given him her business line. She received so few personal calls, she wasn't even used to giving out that number.

"Hello, Fantasy?" Victor noticed immediately how high the pitch of his voice sounded to his own ears. He quickly cleared his throat and spoke again much more deeply. "Is this Fantasy Whitman?"

"Hello, Victor." Her heart began to pound against her chest. She couldn't believe that he sounded the same after all these years. He, of course, was trying to mask the pitch of his voice, but there was no mistaking it; the person on the other end of the line was Victor.

"It's so good to finally get a chance to talk to you." There was a sudden rush of heat and he fanned himself with a nearby piece of paper.

"It's good to get a chance to talk to you too." Hold up, wait a minute, she thought. She was embarrassed already. Hearing his voice had reduced her to sounding like a mockingbird, as if someone were instructing her to repeat after him.

"There's so much I want to say. So much I need to say," Victor began.

"Victor, as I said in my message, let's let all that go. We were young then." Fantasy removed her glasses and rubbed her eyes. "Now that we are much older I think we should use this time to just build a foundation for a new beginning." She didn't really believe that, but she had to admit that it sounded good.

"I'm all for that. But, before we can move on, I just have to tell you how sorry I am. You deserve to know what happened. Not just what you heard, but the honest truth. I owe you that." Victor felt a little emotional.

I am owed more than that, she thought. "In time. Right now just tell me about Command Chief Master Sergeant Victor Charles. That sounds so impressive."

"Thank you for that compliment." Victor smiled, liking the way his title sounded coming out of her mouth.

He began to tell her all about his wing and all that they did. After more than ten minutes, he realized he had been going on and on. "Fantasy, I've talked enough about me. Why don't you tell me about what you do?"

Even though she didn't know when, at some point Fantasy had closed her eyes and just listened to Victor. She didn't really hear or comprehend all that he said or what she answered periodically. It just felt so soothing to listen to him. There were a few times when his voice went up slightly high, but she ascribed that to Victor's nerves. Consumed in their conversation he had become more relaxed and obviously confident in what he was sharing, because his voice was slow and deep.

"There really isn't much to tell. I work for a local newspaper in the sales department." What a lie. She planned to never give him her work number, nor would she give him too much information about the paper she was supposed to work for. Of course, she was a very popular syndicated news journalist, but she solely did print. They thought it would provoke great media hype to have her avoid photo ops and all television exposure. There were a few in the industry who could put name and face together, but to the outside world Jordan Alexander was a faceless newswoman.

"Oh, that sounds interesting. Do you like it?" Victor was interested. He didn't care what she did for a living. He knew from her college days that she was a bright girl. Her profile page only said she was in media; obviously she didn't feel comfortable sharing where she was on the workforce totem pole. Who knew exactly what detours her life had taken after she left college? He had tried to sever all the ties that connected him to the world they had once shared, hoping it would hurt less.

"It pays the bills." Fantasy looked around her home office, visually went beyond those walls to the rest of her stylish and immaculate home, and frowned. She hadn't just paid the bills since she finished graduate school. Fantasy was living rather large.

"You have any kids?" Victor quizzed.

Fantasy gave a quick response. "No." There was the second lie. She would have pinched herself if she didn't think she would yell out, "ouch." Hopefully none of this would come back to bite her. The fact was that if she was going to carry out her plan, all of this prep work was necessary.

"Oh, okay. Well, Sonya and I have a daughter, Niya Rae. She's a senior at Duke University."

Fantasy dropped the pad she was holding. "Where does she attend again?" She couldn't believe what she was hearing.

"Duke. She's a dual major and plans on going to medical school next fall. She would have graduated by now, but she took a year off to travel abroad."

What great news, Fantasy thought. His daughter with Sonya traveled abroad. If she had on a collar she would surely be hot under it, but, as it was, she was more than warm all over. "What a wonderful experience. I've heard great things about Duke." She chuckled nervously.

His daughter and Kam were at Duke at the same time. What were the odds that the two, brother and sister, would end up on the same campus? Her mind raced. What if they knew each other? She rewound several conversations she'd had with Kam regarding school. A few times she paused, trying to figure out if she had heard Kam mention a girl named Niya.

"Well, she does well there. She's a very beautiful girl and I'm extremely proud of her." Not wanting to rub it in or irritate Fantasy, he suddenly stopped talking. The truth that Niya's mother was someone else had to make his past love interest uneasy. He quickly recovered and changed the subject. "So where's home for you these days? I know you mentioned North Carolina in one of your messages."

She had thought about that in preparation for the conversation she knew they would have. "Oh, Durham." That should be safe. It was the only question that she had sort of answered in truth, since she had actually lived in Durham with her grandparents. Hopefully this one tidbit of correct information would counteract at least one of the things she colorfully fixed up to avoid the honest-to-God truth.

"I remember that's where you grew up too, right?" He did remember that from long ago.

"Yes," said Fantasy.

"All those times I was in your neck of the woods and I never ran into you." He couldn't believe it.

"Yeah." That was the only thing that Fantasy could say. There may have even been a time when they were both on the campus, visiting their kids. She opened a nearby bottle of water and took a big drink, wishing it were something stronger, like a Dr. Pepper. This revelation was too much. Thank God she didn't indulge in alcoholic beverages, or the minute she hung up it would have been Miller time.

"I am really enjoying talking to you," Victor said.

"I am too. But as much as I'm enjoying talking, Victor, I have to go. I almost forgot that I have an appointment." She knew she had to end this conversation and regroup. "This is actually the first day I've had off in a while."

"Oh, okay. I understand." Victor didn't want to end their conversation. "I hope I'm not being too forward, but I'm hoping you will give me the chance to get to know you again." He paused, trying not to come on too strong. "From the time I got your message, I've had a good feeling about this, about us." Victor listened as Luther began to fill the background with his sultry sound.

Fantasy regained enough composure to pick up her act. "I feel real good about us too. I'm thinking we should consider all the possibilities."

"Really?" Victor couldn't believe that things were falling into place. He hadn't even shared all of what he'd planned, and, most of all, he hadn't told her what had happened back then.

"Yes, really." She laughed lightly. He sounded like a child who had been told that he could have new toy. "Victor, I'm at a point in my life where I'm looking for a perfect ending. We began so well, I guess I can't help but wonder what life would be like if we had another chance." She rubbed her temple. This conversation was sure to give her a headache.

"That sounds so wonderful." Remembering that she had to go, he spoke up. "Well, can we talk again soon? How often do you go out of town?"

The chore for Fantasy would be keeping up with the script. She had told him she had been out of town, and someone in sales wouldn't be going out of town all that often. "Oh, that was for a conference. I rarely go out of town." She was going to have to back into the church. All this lying would keep her from even walking through the door with her head held high.

"Okay. Well, you have my numbers. I'm usually home after seven P.M., unless I have a meeting or some affair. Then there is e-mail and Facebook." He laughed. "What I'm saying is please feel free to contact me anytime you like."

"I will. It was great talking with you, Victor."

"Fantasy, I do mean anytime. There is so much but it will come later. I'll talk with you again real soon. Goodbye."

When he put the phone down, he leaned his head back against the sofa. He felt like crying. In fact, a few times while they had gone back and forth, he did shed a tear. She should have been his wife. He felt that Fantasy should have been the one. While he listened to her tonight, Victor heard a faint voice whisper her name, not once, but twice. He heard a still, small voice. When he strained to hear the whisper, it fell clearly on his ears, and the whisper said, "Fantasy." He sat straight up and looked around. It was clear, and he understood perfectly what was said.

Victor spoke out loud. "Don't tell me it's that easy. Don't tell me it's been Fantasy all along."

Chapter 9

Saturday had been spent going to yard sales, one of her nana's favorite pastimes, and they had visited her mother's grave for her birthday. Fantasy had not forgotten that it was her mother's birthday, but she had not traveled home specifically to visit the grave. Her grandmother made a point of visiting the grave often to make sure it was kept up and to place flowers there on a regular basis. While her nana stood there and softly hummed with tears in her eyes, Fantasy held her grandmother's hand tightly and looked down solemnly. She felt very little; nothing that would move her to tears.

They walked back to the car hand in hand. "Nana, I have a great idea for the next few hours of our girls' day out." She smiled, wanting to do something to lighten the moment. Fantasy felt guilty that she didn't and couldn't feel anything, but what she did feel was her grandmother's pain.

"What do you have in mind?" Pearl squeezed Fantasy's hand, grateful to have a piece of her Valerie. She treasured Fantasy as her only grandchild, but also because she was all she had left of her only child.

"We are going to the spa. And before you turn your lips upside down, I will not take no for an answer." She opened the car locks and helped her grandmother into the front passenger seat.

"Listen to you being bossy. You know I have never been interested in nobody touching on this old body." She chuckled. "I'll leave the massaging to Matthew."

"Okay. That's nice. For today, though, we are going to let a professional give your body some attention. It's such a wonderful experience. I've been trying to get you to go for so long. So today, please go just for me. And I'll be on the table right beside you." She looked at her Nana and pouted her lip.

"You are too much. All right, Fantasy, let's go to the spa then." Pearl fastened her seat beat. "Lord, have mercy on this old soul."

Fantasy winked at her. "He will."

It felt good to be in her home church. The stained-glass windows were so beautiful and resonant of an old-fashioned, stately, traditional church. The current edifice had been there for 130 years. Three generations of the Whitman family had been proud to call Zion Baptist their church home.

Fantasy had spent most every Sunday there, from the time she'd moved there until she went away to college in Virginia. The only interruption she had in attending church was illness, and even then she had to be close to coughing up a lung or enduring a fever well over 101 degrees. Only one time had she witnessed both her grandparents in bed, sick. They had both come down with the flu. Fantasy had skipped around all Saturday evening, talking on the phone and waiting on them between television shows. When she went to bed well after midnight, she'd assumed she would have the luxury of sleeping in. That was not the case. Her nana woke her up at 7:00 and told her that their neighbor, Ms. Abbie, would be picking her up for Sunday School and Sunday service, and she would drop her off after everything was over. In short, Fantasy was almost never allowed to miss church. It was hard to get used to in the beginning, since she didn't attend regularly with her mother, but she'd adjusted and had come to admire and appreciate what her grandparents imparted, and the importance of attending a place of worship.

Nick and Kam were seated on both sides of Fantasy. She was sure that a lot of people probably thought that Nick was her man. He had joined her at church more than a few times, and each time she saw the envious looks she got from the females who, she knew, couldn't stand her. Most of them were still locals and hadn't done much with their lives. The fact that she had a career and her return visits to her church home showed that visibly she had it going on, that alone was enough to cause her to get major hate from them. Then, on occasion, she would waltz into church with the likes of Nick, who showered her with major attention the entire time. Little did they know he was focused on his best friend because he was in the Lord's house, and out of respect he didn't use this sacred place to pursue women. Pearl and Matthew didn't even think about telling the church folk that Nick and Fantasy were just friends because, in their words, "it was nobody's business."

The church wasn't as packed as it normally was. Only the center floor pews held parishioners. Fantasy looked around, and smiled and waved at a few of the older members. She was dressed in a white short-sleeved fitted blazer suit with turquoise-and-rhinestone-accented ankle-wrap sandals. Her necklace was made of multicolored watercolor beads, and she wore matching earrings. She opted to let her hair hang, and it curved slightly to frame her face. It was a simple style, and yet Fantasy was radiant and so well put together. She possessed a classy appeal, and her presence always made a statement without her having to open her mouth.

Pearl sat proudly with the other missionaries in their assigned two pews in the front. Matthew was already situated in his honorary spot: the first row, second seat of the deacon's stand. He was the second oldest deacon, and, while no one really said so, their seating order went from the oldest to the youngest. He sat there with his chest puffed out and looking all regal, as if Paul and the other disciples were seated among him and his fellow deacons. You couldn't tell Matthew Whitman that he wasn't doing the Lord's work; he'd likely cuss you and invite you outside for more than a conversation.

Pastor Johns stood up just as the young adult choir finished singing an upbeat, nontraditional song. Times had changed at Zion, and so had the music.

"Good morning, saints of God." His voice boomed through the sound system. "I said, good morning, saints." The congregation responded in semi-unison.

"It's so good to be in the house of the Lord one more time. He didn't have to let me live, I said, He didn't have to let me live, but I'm so glad that He did." He threw his head back as if that had all come as an epiphany.

Fantasy giggled to herself. Her grandmother was right: he needed to step it up a notch. That was the same opening he had been giving since she moved to Durham. There had to be something else he could say, some other greeting that lay heavily on his heart.

He continued, "This Sunday morning we going to follow up with our Sunday School theme and talk about forgiveness."

Nick looked over at Fantasy. "The pastor is getting ready to talk about forgiveness. You may want to take some notes."

Fantasy narrowed her eyes at Nick. "Whatever." She twisted in her seat. She couldn't believe that of all the Sundays for her to visit her home church, she would be joining in to hear a sermon about forgiveness. It just happened to be the one thing she was struggling with. Here she was planning the ultimate revenge, when she really needed to let go and let God.

"Turn with me to John 3:16 and listen to what it says. 'For God so loved the world that He gave His only begotten Son, that whoever believes in Him should not perish but have everlasting life.'" Pastor Johns raised his hand up. "That's a rich Word, if you just think about what the good Lord is telling us. But we can't fully understand, get that scripture down in our spirits, and receive the promise, unless we forgive those who have wronged us."

Several in the congregation gave refrains of "Amen." A few waved their hands, motioning that he was obviously preaching right.

"If you don't forgive others, how do you expect Him to forgive you?"

Fantasy squirmed again. That statement alone had her rethinking her plan. She was pulled into a state of uncertainty. Right after he talked about little white lies and about untruths having a snowball effect, she tuned out everything else that Pastor Johns preached about.

By the time he finished the sermon, and had altar call and offering, Fantasy felt like a heel and totally convicted. Just the day before she'd had another conversation with Victor, and she was pouring it on thick. He seemed to be enjoying what she was saying, and she was enjoying his reaction to what she was saying, while she was trying hard not to. No good could come of her allowing any of it to touch her deep down.

"So how did you enjoy the service today, Fantasy?"

She was helping her grandmother set the table. The meal was already prepared down to the desserts.

"It was good. I enjoyed it." Fantasy carried the last serving platter and placed it on the overcrowded buffet table. "Nick and I always get plenty of attention whenever we show up. I must say, my best friend looks good on my arm." She smiled, knowing it was the truth.

"I know. I was watching. It's humorous to me that folks are so nosey. Nobody at that church minds their own business. I was asked by a few if he was your significant other, and I didn't answer one way or the other. The thing is, they ask me that every single time you two come home. I just changed the subject and kept right on 'bout my business." Pearl poured gravy from a steaming hot pan into the gravy bowl.

"Good for you, Nana," said Fantasy.

"But, you know, you and Nick make a cute couple. I can see why people young and old would think you two are together."

"Nana, we've been through this before. Nick and I are just friends. It would be like being with a brother." She frowned. The thought of being with Nick always made her feel really funny. "We are just that close."

"Sometimes that makes the best relationship. You two know everything about each other. There probably isn't one secret between you two," Pearl added.

"You're right. We know everything there is to know about each other. Some of it is abbreviated but it's all been shared. It's funny, out of all the female friends I've ever had, Nick and I share a special bond. I feel confident that he will always have my back." Fantasy stopped what she was doing and thought about just how close she was to Nick. "Of course, Kam is my heart, but Nick is closer to me than anyone, except for you." Fantasy, with a big smile, reached over and touched her grandmother on the hand.

"I'm your girl, that's for sure." Pearl tried to sound young and hip. "Speaking of being your girl, that massage was the bomb."

"I could tell you enjoyed it. I called your name a few times and all I could hear was a snore." Fantasy laughed hard.

"Child, that put me right to sleep." Pearl moved around the table. "But back to what we were talking about. Is Nick seeing anyone?" Pearl was determined to make a love connection and be nosey at the same time.

"Yes. I think he likes her a lot."

Nick had continued to see Dee since that night at AJ's. Fantasy had even caught a movie with them a few nights ago. Fantasy thought he would need therapy to deal with the hair situation, but he seemed fine with it. He was even going to work up the nerve to ask her about her own hair, thinking that maybe she had long hair or good hair and had just gotten used to wearing weaves. Whatever the outcome, he seemed to like her, and continued to share that he would not be exiting just because of hair or lack thereof. "And you, sweetie, are you seeing someone?" Pearl asked as she wiped her hands on her apron.

Fantasy thought about what was starting between her and Victor. It wasn't a relationship and, therefore, not worth mentioning. It would be over almost before it really began. That was the plan, a plan she was determined to stick to. "No, I just don't have time."

Just then, Matthew came into the dining room with Kam and Nick right behind him. "We couldn't stand the wonderful smells coming from this room one moment longer. Me and these boys are hungry and ready to chow down."

"We were just about ready to call you. Why don't you all go and wash your hands." Pearl beamed over her nicely set table. Everything looked so elegant and the food smelled heavenly.

"We already took care of that." Matthew Whitman took his seat at the head of the table.

Kam and everyone else took their usual seats. Once everyone was positioned all around the table, Pearl nodded toward Matthew. "Go ahead and bless the food, honey."

"Sure, buttercup," Matthew said.

Fantasy grimaced, thinking about her conversation with her nana, the one about the little blue pills. The thought of him popping a pill and romancing her grandmother was something she didn't need to even think about. Whatever Matthew did, Pearl loved it, and they were still in awe of one another. They were happy and that was all that mattered.

"Lord, we are thankful for this time of family coming together. Oh, Mighty God, we appreciate this wonderful meal that has been prepared. Bless the hands that labored in its preparation, and allow it to provide nourishment for our physical bodies. In all things we give thanks. In the precious name of your son, Jesus, we pray. Amen."

Everyone followed in unison by saying, "Amen."

Dinner conversation was easy and it flowed from one topic to another.

"Nick, I'm glad you decided to join us on our fishing excursion," said Matthew.

"I'm glad you didn't mind me tagging along," Nick responded, and handed his plate to Fantasy so she could place on it what she knew he liked.

"Of course not. You are family." Matthew reached for a roll. "You have a standing invitation to join this family for any affair or activity."

"Pop, we beat the bricks off Deacon Scott and his two sons." Kam laughed as he reached for the basket of rolls his grandfather extended.

"I know, Kam. He's been bragging about them getting the trophy for catching the most fish last year," Matthew added. "This year we took both trophies home with us."

"They assumed that Nick didn't know a hook from a rod," said Kam.

"They didn't ask. If they did, I would have told them I've been fishing since I was old enough to hold a rod. My great-grandfather was a waterman on the eastern shore. It's in my blood," Nick said.

"Well, thank God for the blood." Matthew laughed.

"Matthew," Pearl said before joining her husband and everyone else who was laughing.

Laughter and wonderful, happy sounds continued to fill the room. It was so apparent that within the walls of the Whitman home was love, and those who joined together to share the bounty of food that spilled off the table were elated to be in each other's company. They feasted on pot roast with gravy, fried chicken, fried clam fritters, mashed potatoes, green peas, corn pudding, and homemade rolls. Lemon meringue pie and German chocolate cake were situated at the end of the buffet table on elegant crystal dessert plates, ready to be consumed.

Fantasy attempted to answer at all the right times and hoped that she said all the right things, but her mind was on her next conversation with Victor. She was so tempted to excuse herself and check her e-mail. Each day since their phone conversation, he sent her at least two e-mails. There were times when an e-mail would come with only a few words, saying that she was in his thoughts, and other times it was pages. She read each word over and over, realizing that he was baring his soul. Still, she would not allow him to tell her the entire story. She told herself that it didn't matter. She wanted her plan to remain intact. However, lately she felt she was ready to hear it; she needed to hear it.

"Earth to Fantasy." Nick leaned over and spoke just loud enough to get her attention. "What time are you talking to Victor?" He pushed up his sleeve and looked at his watch.

"What?" She looked in the direction of his voice and tried to focus. "Victor? What are you talking about?"

"You are on edge and it seems you are ready to hit the back room so you can check your phone. Just wondered if he was calling today." Nick continued to lean in with a grin. He knew her so well.

"I was not thinking about talking to him. You know the plan." Fantasy had shared with Nick each time she talked to Victor. She sort of needed him to help her stay on task.

"I do. I also know that you still care."

"Whatever, Nick. That may be, but I'm sticking with the plan. Nothing else matters. Absolutely nothing," Fantasy responded. She needed to convince herself more than she needed to convince Nick.

At that moment, her eyes moved across the table to Kam. She had been staring at him ever since she picked him up from the airport. Fantasy's eyes took in every feature, as if she needed to recommit them all to memory. It wasn't really necessary; she knew every one well. He could pass for Victor's twin. She wondered if Victor came face to face with Kam, whether he would be able to see himself in Kam.

Nick followed her eyes, and since he had seen the recent photos on Facebook, and she had finally shared a few of the college photos she had, he connected the dots. "Yeah, he does."

Fantasy looked at Nick, shocked at what he'd just said. "What?"

"Kam looks just like him," Nick answered without blinking.

"How did you know?" Her eyes welled with tears that were ready to fall. "I never said . . ." The rest of her words drifted into silence.

"We'll talk later. This isn't the time or the place." He reached under the table for her hand, wanting to reassure her. "Your secret is safe."

"I know." Her eyes had to speak the admiration she held for their closeness. So many times she'd wanted to tell Nick, but decided to carry the burden alone.

"What are you two talking about?" Kam stopped talking to his grandfather and looked in their direction.

"Nothing much. I was just telling Nick how handsome you are." In saying that he was handsome, it meant that Victor was just as handsome.

"That I already know. Unless I've gotten more handsome since I've been in DC." Kam rubbed his hand over his goatee and grinned.

Just then the doorbell rang. He had been waiting for Brittany, who was at a late church service with her parents. He jumped up and bolted out of the room. Everyone at the table busted out laughing.

Matthew was the first to speak. "Young love. I remember when Pearl had me running like that."

"If you could move that fast you would still be running." Pearl winked at him.

"You know that's right, honey. You a whole lot of wonderful woman to run after." Matthew leaned toward his wife.

"Okay. I think I'm going to be sick." Fantasy joked at her grandparents' love antics. They had been so expressive in their love lately. It had to have been the blue pills.

Nick spoke up. "I think it's so sweet. Mr. Matthew, I think I may have met someone special. The next time we come down I'm going to bring her."

Fantasy smiled in agreement.

Pearl answered before her husband could. "We'd like that a lot."

All eyes were on Fantasy. She stuffed a piece of lemon meringue pie in her mouth and looked up. "What? As soon as I get a whole lot of wonderful man, I'll be sure to bring him by."

"Hello, everybody." Brittany came in holding Kam's hand.

Everyone spoke and she took a few minutes going around the table hugging and kissing everyone's cheeks.

"Have something to eat. There is plenty." Pearl got up to fix Brittany a plate.

"Actually, I will have a little." She smiled nervously.

"Well, actually, Nana, if you don't mind, we'd like to tell you guys something before she starts to eat."

Fantasy looked at her son and her stomach dropped. She knew that they had gone against her advice to wait, and had been doing a whole lot of everything. She held her breath and prayed to God that it was not what she thought. She didn't want his life to be interrupted. Brittany was a nice girl, and she was pleased with his choice. But this was no time for them to be pregnant. She wasn't ready to be a grandmother.

All eyes were on Kam as he grabbed Brittany's left hand and slowly placed it on the table. "We are engaged."

No one said a word for a few moments. Kam eyed each of them, trying to gauge what they were thinking. He felt like he was in front of a firing squad.

Pearl was the first to snap out of the moment and react. She got up, went over to the young couple, and hugged them both tightly. "This is so wonderful. I'm so happy for you two." Matthew was next with hugs and a big kiss on the cheek for Brittany. Nick did the same. All the while, Fantasy was frozen in her seat. She was unable to move and still held her fork in midair.

Brittany looked like she was about to cry. She loved Kam, and she worked hard on having a relationship with his mother. Fantasy was pleasant, but she often felt it was forced. It was understandable; Kam was her only child and he had a bright future in front of him. The truth was that Kam wasn't the only one; she was going to have a great career, and together they would have a wonderful life. It was important to both of them not to rely on the resources of her parents or his mother. She had been born into a well-to-do family and never wanted for anything, and neither did Kam. But that didn't stop them from wanting their own together.

"Mom." Kam stood up and walked over to his mother. He pulled her up out of her seat and watched the tears well in her eyes. "Please don't cry."

Fantasy tried to stop. "I'm happy for you, Kam. This is just hard."

"Mom, Brittany and I have talked about this. I would never turn my back on you. You aren't losing me, you could never lose me. In fact, you are gaining a daughter, and, after a while, you will be gaining grandkids. You have raised me well with the help of Nana and Granddad. You have sacrificed and gone above and beyond because my father has never been involved. I never understand why he didn't want me, and I could never tell you that. After a while it didn't matter to me, because God had blessed me with a wonderful family. Then, in addition to Granddad, Nick came along and I had another positive man in my life. Things have not been bad at all and I want to share this family, my family, with the love of my life."

Fantasy could only nod. There were no words right now that would support what she felt, and she wasn't exactly feeling what everybody else was feeling right this minute.

"I don't know if you have ever been in love. I'd like to believe that you loved the man who is my father. If that's the case, you'd know how I feel about Brittany."

By the time he finished his speech, everybody—including Nick, as hard as he tried to compose himself—was crying.

"I know what it's like, and I would never want you to live without the one you love." Fantasy thought of Victor and another tear fell. "Brittany, welcome to the family." As soon as the words were out of Fantasy's mouth, Brittany squealed. She jumped up, ran around the table, and hugged them both.

They were in love. Just the two of them. There was no love triangle and her son was not competing with anyone for the number one spot in Brittany's life. If he was, no one was the wiser. They were totally consumed with each other.

Fantasy was not an advocate of love for obvious reasons. Because she loved her son, she wouldn't let that hinder what he wanted. She had to believe that love on the right terms, with all the right ingredients, was possible, and that it didn't have to end badly.

"I love you. Now, if everyone will excuse me for a few minutes, I'm going to have a moment." Fantasy hiccupped through a few tears and laughed. She really did understand, and was going to be totally supportive. Still, everyone had to know that it was difficult to allow her hands to open freely and allow her son to soar on his own without her to guard his landing. Kam was a grown man and this day and his decision to marry really proved that he wouldn't be needing her as much, if at all. Contrary to all he said to make her feel better, Brittany would be his go-to woman.

Again, Pearl was the first to recognize what was needed. "You go right ahead, sweetie. Kam can keep Brittany company while she eats her dinner and Nick can help me clean up. Your grandfather will be retiring to the living room. According to his normal after-dinner clock, he's only a few minutes from snooze land." She chuckled, and so did everyone else, knowing how true her words were.

"Woman, you think you know me." Matthew got up from the table, grabbed the Sunday paper, and walked toward the living room. He mumbled as he went along. "I'm going watch a little golf, read the paper, and just enjoy myself. I might close my eyes for a few minutes but I won't fall asleep."

Right after her grandfather left the room, Fantasy walked through the dining room, then through the kitchen and out the back door. The weather was seasonably hot. The ending of the month of August was nearing and there were the marked winds that alerted all those natives to the southeast that storms were nearing on the coast. Those winds cooled things down just a little and made this the perfect climate.

She sat down on the porch swing and looked around the yard. The little girl who had come here in total rage a lifetime ago, feeling that she knew it all and possessing a huge chip on her shoulder, had, in time, softened. Her grandparents had given her time, love, and reassurance, and neither grandparent kept records of all the wrongs, but they so quickly pointed out all the rights. Even when she came with the news that she was pregnant, they embraced her and announced that together they would rear her seed, and even though it wasn't planned, it was a blessing. Nana added that God was giving them a chance to give love out of the abundance they had. She had also said that God was giving her one more person to love in addition to loving her. They'd made the best of that situation, and Kam was their jewel.

She removed her iPhone from her pocket and checked her e-mail, as she knew there would be a message there from Victor. She opened it and started to read:

Hello, Fantasy. I can't begin to tell you how happy these past weeks have been. I go to bed at night thinking that I'll wake up and it will all be a dream, then the next day begins and I realize that it's not a dream. You are real and this is real. I'm simply elated and so very happy. You have asked questions and allowed me to share my world as if anything about me is interesting. There is one thing that I'm wondering: what is it that you remember the most after all this time? For me it's easy. I remember what an extraordinary woman you were then, and to know that she has remained is so mind-blowing. Even before we talked by phone you had already given me something I so desperately needed. It was as if you came into my life totally in touch, and you gave me what I needed the most: hope. I am so in debt to you as I have always been. I know this may be difficult to understand, and you may not even have the capacity to believe me, God knows you have your reasons, but you have always brought me joy, and now a contentment that I never thought possible. Forever, Victor

She smiled. It was a nice e-mail. He must have really thought he was saying all the right things and assumed it was exactly what she wanted to hear. She felt like a two-sided coin because part of her wanted to receive and accept what he had shared, and the other side felt it was still too little, too late. Fantasy couldn't help being perplexed about Victor. She was anything but stupid and naïve, and she would be both if she just bought what he said and accepted this man at face value. There was a need to rein in what could be viewed as the brink of anger at being considered so gullible. She inhaled and slowly exhaled. She repeated the process a few more times, and then she began to respond to his e-mail:

I don't mind you sharing. I think your life is very interesting. You have so much to be thankful for, and, although I have no right to be, I am very proud of all that you have accomplished. What a tremendous blessing. What is it that I remember? I remember July '83 very well. It was the last time I saw you and we spent the evening together. I don't expect you to remember that, but I do. I remember the special dinner, the walk. Victor, I recall our laughter that came so easily, and, most of all, I remember what we started. And because I remember all that, I can't help but remember the calls I waited for and the days I waited for you to stroll through campus just to see me. To somehow pick up where we left off. When none of that came to be, I remember how hard it was for me to let you go.

Fantasy stopped for a second, not wanting to dwell on the bad. She took a deep breath and continued.

But when I sent you a message and you responded, I realized that maybe, just maybe, we were given another chance. You were special, so I had to reach back and pull us out of the past long enough to envision what my future could have been. I hope this makes sense. Until we talk again, Fantasy

Pleased with her response, Fantasy returned her thoughts to Kam. Somehow, though, she wasn't able to switch the tables just that quick. What was more evident was that, although she was trying, she wasn't able to put thoughts of Victor aside so easily.

Chapter 10

Victor walked around the small apartment with the cordless phone to his ear. He had been talking to Fantasy for more than an hour. Today had been another early home day. He didn't have a heavy schedule, and when an onset of nausea and vomiting hit him, he cancelled all that was on his calendar and went home to rest. It had to be some bug. Whatever it was, it had him feeling rotten. "I know, Fantasy. I'm going to warm some soup and rest the minute I hang up the phone." He smiled at her concern.

"I think you should." She was in the mall, looking for the right shoes to accent the outfit she would wear at the after-five charity event that was being cosponsored by her company.

"I just don't want to hang up the phone. And there's something I wanted to ask you." Victor had been thinking, since he'd received the information a few days ago, that this would be a great opportunity to see her.

Fantasy picked up a designer shoe in Saks, and tilted it from side to side. "Please ask, and then you can hang up." She was a little worried about him not feeling well lately. Plan or not, she didn't want anything happening to him.

"I'm on TDY in Washington, DC in two weeks, and I really would like you to meet me, or, if you prefer, I can come there to see you." He held his breath and waited for her to say something.

"Really?" She had thought about her plan progressing to the point that they would meet. So, in retrospect, this was all going better than she thought it would. "That would be great. I'd love to meet you there. E-mail your details and I'll see if I can take a few days off from work."

"I don't want you to take time off from work if it will be a hassle. I can drive there, or, better yet, I can route my flight there for a few extra days."

"That won't be necessary. I'll ask when I go back after my lunch break. It's slow, so it shouldn't be a problem." Fantasy knew all too well that she could adjust her schedule at will. She had worked so hard that, until recently, she had been glued to her desk and always working on something. It seemed that more and more lately she was looking at life through a different-colored lens, a lens that did not include her working herself to exhaustion. Her medical appointment would be the next day, and she hoped that they could give her something for the pain that was not managed by her previous medicine. There had to be something else that could possibly help. It was a long shot, but she was hoping for something that would require only a slight adjustment to her lifestyle.

Victor couldn't believe she was agreeing. He thought that he would have to twist her arm, and yet she agreed willingly. A little out of it, he sat down and wiped his forehead with the back of his hand. "Well, we can plan things later. Take care." He wanted to add that he loved her, but didn't want to say too much too soon. Too many things hadn't been said, and, while he knew they were both working on a solid foundation of getting to know each other, there was still some uncertainty.

"Okay. I'll talk to you soon." Fantasy disconnected the call and turned to look for a salesperson.

Before Victor could hang the phone up, it rang again. He smiled, thinking it was Fantasy calling back to give him one more remedy to try. He had talked to Niya before he'd left work. There had been a few financial issues he'd needed to handle with the school, and if it meant he could avoid talking to Sonya, he would have called Satan. "Hello."

"Command Chief Charles, this is Dr. Knapp."

Victor looked at his watch, thinking that the medical facility closed at 5:00. "Yes, Dr. Knapp, you must have some information for me."

"I do, Chief. I was wondering if you could come in tomorrow morning." He paused. "You can come in anytime before noon. Just tell the receptionist you need to see me."

"This must be real important." Victor wanted to see if the doctor would give him a clue as to what was going on. "I mean, just giving the word and being able to see you just like that without an appointment."

"I assure you it's nothing that hasn't been done before." The doctor tried to reassure him and to limit sounding a health problem alarm. That was never good for any patient. This call itself was likely sending up a flag. Dr. Knapp knew that if he began to talk about the results, Victor would have questions that shouldn't be answered over the phone.

"Can you tell me what is going on? What did the test results show?" Victor knew that the doctor was trying to avoid revealing anything over the phone.

"I'd rather see you in the office. That way, if there are questions, we can talk about them at length."

"Well, okay. I'll be in tomorrow." He hung up the phone. How was he supposed to rest tonight? The doctor had discovered something that warranted making another visit to the medical facility, and that had him concerned. He sat there in a chair, sweating like it was hotter than hot when the apartment was only slightly warm.

There was a knock on the door. Hardly anyone ever came over to his apartment, and if someone did he always knew in advance. As close as he and Darryl were, they never dropped by each other's place unannounced. In Darryl's case, Victor never knew when he was entertaining company, and in his case, Darryl just respected his privacy. As he sat there, confused about who it could be, whoever it was knocked again. Victor went to the door and opened it without question.

Lopez stood at the door. "Hello, Chief. I'm sorry to drop by unannounced, but there are some reports that need a response by morning and I thought I'd drop them off on the way home."

"You didn't have to go to all that trouble. All you needed to do was call and I would have gone back by the office and looked over them." Victor opened the folder with a puzzled look on his face. He was certain that he had gone over everything earlier in the day before he left the office. There was nothing pending, and no one had mentioned needing a response to anything else, not even the general. He never looked up at her, but continued to glance through the pages.

"It was no trouble." She was still standing at the door. Lopez thought that if she showed up at the door with some urgent paperwork, he would have at least invited her in and thanked her profusely for ensuring that nothing fell through the cracks. Yet, he had her standing outside.

"Thanks a lot. I'll check these out and drop them off in the morning. I have an appointment so I should be in and out before you get there. Depending on how my appointment goes, I may or may not be in after that." He closed the folder and looked at her closely for the first time since he swung the door open.

"Oh. Is everything okay? I know you have been very distracted. Is there anything I can do, anything at all that I can help you with?" She leaned forward.

Victor noticed that her shirt was open a little lower than it normally was when they were in the office. He was a little slow when it came to advances, so his ex-wife used to tell him, but it was hard to miss what Lopez was up to. "I am fine, and I don't need a thing. As I said, I'll leave these on your desk. Thanks again." Victor was about to close the door when she walked closer to him.

"Chief, I will do anything to help you." She boldly traced her manicured nail up his arm and licked her lips.

"Lopez, you are out of order, and I'm going to ask you to leave." He took two steps back. "And once you are away from my door and out of sight, I'm going to pretend that this, whatever it is, never happened." He was upset and wanted to say so much more. Victor would need time to reflect to see if at any time he could have sent a message to Lopez that would have led to this. He didn't think so, but for the record, and since it was a serious matter, he'd go back over everything.

Lopez didn't move right away. "I have been thinking about how lonely you must be, and you don't have to, because I am more than available. If you are worried that I'd openly display any affection toward you, I wouldn't. I know your position requires that you be secretive. I can do that, Chief." Again she touched his arm, and this time she moved in so close, her breast rubbed against him.

"That's it. Leave my apartment immediately. I'm going to have you reassigned. In the meantime, I am requesting that you do just your job, nothing more and nothing less." He moved around her and stood at the door, making no eye contact.

Without a word, she walked out the door and glanced back at him with a sick smirk that he could not understand. Victor had asked her to leave immediately and had informed her that she would be reassigned. She had to know that the powers that be would question why. He could tell them the truth or create a story that they didn't work together well. It happened often. The difference was that Victor never had a problem getting along with anyone. Lopez would be the first. Yes, subordinates had come on to him, but never so forwardly, and not one of them was so adamant that risking their positions was a concern.

"I'll see you in the office." She touched her butt as she walked away.

Victor watched as she turned the corner, and then she was out of sight. He closed the door and rubbed his hand over his face. He knew he needed to document exactly what had happened. There was always the chance that she could put her own spin on things. That was the last thing he needed. Victor had never been faced with anyone questioning him of unethical behavior. Still, if Lopez was so out of touch that she couldn't take his no for an answer, it was hard to say what lengths she would go to. He was so sure when he opened the door that her visit was on the up and up. If he had thought that she had any other agenda than dropping off some files, he would have dismissed her immediately. How many classes had he had concerning related incidents?

He thought about calling Darryl, but decided to tell him later. He needed to lie down. This had been a crazy day. Victor closed the curtain in his bedroom and looked around for the remote. When he found it, he clicked on the television and wasn't even concerned about what was on. He just needed the noise.

He got into the bed and stretched out. It felt good just to allow his body to hit the soft mattress. The 500-thread-count Egyptian cotton sheets felt so good against his skin. This was another one of those requirements he had that might seem petty to some, but sleeping on high-thread-count sheets was a must for him. It wasn't like he was ever planning on broadcasting this particular like, nor did he plan on sharing his preference just like that. Maybe he would, if it meant that he was about to be sharing his bed with someone.

The thought of sharing his bed caused him to think of Fantasy. They had talked countless times, yet still she would never agree to Skype with him. She continued to play it off like she didn't know anything about how to get it on her computer. All it took was for her to have a webcam, or pick up one, go to the site, and then follow the directions. Every time he brought it up, she would quickly change the subject. It couldn't have had anything to do with her looks; in the two photos on Facebook she was just as beautiful as she always had been. It was as if time had stood still. Nothing about Fantasy had changed.

Victor slipped farther down in the bed and placed his hands behind his head. He remembered the late night she came over to his apartment back then. They'd hardly talked; instead they spent hours just holding hands and watching a movie. During that time they never even kissed; the two just looked at each other and smiled. The chemistry was so strong and being in her presence was so intoxicating. He was so at ease around her. There were no demands put on his time or what he needed to be for her. All Fantasy wanted was whatever he offered. She'd held his head in her lap and he remembered falling asleep. Victor wasn't sure how long he had slept, but when he'd opened his dazed eyes, the movie had gone off and the late news was on. When he'd looked up, she was wide awake and was simply massaging his temple and rubbing the side of his face. He had never been so comfortable with anyone, and that moment could have lasted forever. He wanted it to last forever. When he did finally kiss her that night, she didn't pull away or act shy just for the sake of it, but she kissed him back. Victor felt something he had never felt before. That entire evening they didn't exchange a lot of conversation; she had come because he was going through some changes with Sonya. That night she'd offered what he needed: a shoulder. Even when the kiss had happened, she immediately apologized and left. She stood at her car and told him with a light touch on his cheek that his friendship meant everything to her, and that as long as he needed her friendship it would always be there. It would never end or have strings attached.

Victor picked up the phone, dialed frantically, and waited.

Fantasy answered her cell phone. "Hello."

"I still love you." Victor knew he was taking a risk and was out of order, considering their pact to work on a solid foundation of friendship first.

Fantasy couldn't believe what she was hearing, what Victor was saying. "Victor."

"Stop. This is not about what you need to say. It's about what I need to say. What I needed to tell you." If this truth and the sharing of it made him a fool, so be it. His mind would race wondering about the results of the medical test, but it wouldn't race with the question of the right time to tell Fantasy that he still loved her.

"Victor." Fantasy spoke his name softly, feeling something deep down that she had vowed to keep locked away.

"No, not now. I just wanted to tell how I feel. Good night, my love." Victor disconnected the line. He smiled a knowing smile. It was difficult to believe that years had passed, and while he went on living what he thought was real, their friendship had remained. There was no reason or rationale why Fantasy had reached out to him, in a Facebook message of all places. She should have gone on with her life back then with no thoughts of him whatsoever, but that wasn't the way life played out. Fantasy had shared in part, but Victor believed there was so much more. He believed that a part of him had been tucked away, and she held on to that part, knowing that time would avail itself again. She had given the sacrifice of time and he had done nothing, nothing to hold on to what they shared until now. He owed her so much. How could he ever repay Fantasy? Victor decided he would do all he could to prove his love, and lavish upon her everything that she deserved. He'd give her all of him.

Yes, Victor thought. He'd give her all of him. Sure, he had vowed after Sonya to give up on love and loving, but for Fantasy he'd take the risk.

When he had exhausted himself mentally with all his thoughts, he closed his eyes and held on to the one that created a place for him and Fantasy. Before long, sleep came.

Chapter 11

Fantasy ran around her bedroom in a frenzy. Her life of order had somehow gone out the window, and if she'd known where it had gone, and in what direction it had traveled, she would have chased it down. She just couldn't seem to get it together. There had been missed deadlines, forgotten meetings, calls not returned. Routine things such as sitting down to handle paying bills were put off until the last possible moment. All of this was so unlike her. She was determined every day to do better and it just wasn't happening. She mentally reversed time to figure out when she started being so absentminded and nonchalant when, in truth, every little thing was a big deal to her. It always had been that way. When success started coming her way and she was accomplishing things that she knew were so out of her reach, she'd worked overtime to make sure all was in place and nothing was ever left to chance. It became her rule of thumb not to let anything fall through the cracks, even if it meant that she reviewed and reviewed.

Just as she was continuing to search for something she couldn't find, Nick walked into the bedroom with the silence of a ninja.

Fantasy got up from on all fours and jumped. "Dag, just scare me to death why don't you?"

"Hey, I thought you heard me walk in." Nick stood with his hands up in the air in defense. He had some prowling skills, but he wasn't using them at the moment.

"I'm sorry, Nick. I know you are here to take me to the airport, and I should have been ready. I just can't find my other shoe." She held up a pewter sling with rhinestone accents across the top.

"Fantasy, you are usually the one texting, phoning, and hassling me about being on time or making you late." He mimicked her voice as he added the last part. "And how is it that you can't find your shoe, your hair is a mess, and you haven't even finished packing?" He just crossed his arms over his chest and began to shake his head. "It's a sad day in Ballantyne Estates when you can't pull it together. Now that information deserves a commentary." Nick chuckled as he mentioned her housing development. It was definitely a neighborhood that only the affluent could afford to live in.

"Stop it, Nick." Fantasy looked at him, totally disappointed in herself. "I know, and I am beside myself. I've been walking around the room talking to myself. This is crazy and it has to stop." They still had plenty of time to make it to the airport, and she would have sufficient time to check in and handle the baggage and security stuff. But her rule was four hours. She sat down on the edge of her bed. "I don't know what's wrong." All of this was driving her up the wall and she was so upset. Some people need to make sense of everything and she was one of them.

Nick began to walk toward her, and, on his way, he picked up the matching shoe she was looking for. When he got to the bed, he plopped down beside her. "Okay, tell me, what do you think is going on? And I really don't think it's all your health." Nick was speaking out of concern. "You do need to go ahead with the reevaluation and see what they are talking about this go-round. Still, there is something else going on and, while I have a clue, I'd rather hear it come out of your mouth."

She listened to her friend and knew he was saying all of the things she had said to herself all morning, the night before, and even the week before. Her version didn't add up. However, hearing it come from Nick, or maybe even just because it was spoken out loud, it made total sense. "Yes, I need to reschedule the medical appointment. This thing with Kam and Brittany, I mean, that hit me out of nowhere. I expected it and yet, in some ways, I didn't. I just don't know, Nick." Fantasy allowed the words to just spill out.

"Good catch, but I really don't think this is about Kam." Nick turned the shoe over and over. "I don't know how you wear these things."

"Give me my shoe." Fantasy took the shoe from him and placed it in the shoe bag with its mate. "You know, from the time I opened that Facebook profile of Victor I've felt out of control. Like I know what I should be doing and saying, but something inside pulls me in another direction. I can't make sense of this."

"And you are not used to not being in control." Nick put emphasis on the word "control" and smiled at her. "Every area of your life is controlled. You have control issues, Fantasy. I love you and feel I can tell you this."

"I'm not even going to lie; I do. I just always want to make sure things are going according to plan," Fantasy said.

"Whose plan?"

"Well, my plan. But, Nick, you know I am fully aware that it's God's plan that matters. Is there anything wrong with helping Him out?" Fantasy asked, knowing that Nick was being a little harsh but it was for her good.

She knew God had a plan and purpose for her life and she was following it, or so she thought. It was just that every now and then she'd reach in and adjust this, that, or the other. They were small adjustments. She didn't do major overhauls, just a few cosmetic alterations. Fantasy saw it as merely accessorizing.

"Flash, boo. He don't need no help. Come on, you know the Word, and you hear recaps of it often enough from Nana and Granddad. Don't even trip," Nick continued. "I think—and this is just my opinion; feel free to go with it or deposit it in the unwanted box—that when this communication thing with Victor started, it was something that was out of your control. I mean, you text or message and he texts or messages. Then, when you two decided to start talking on the phone, there were still so many unknowns, so much uncertainty. The bottom line is that as much as you are trying to run this scheme and you got this plan in the works, you, my friend, are not in control. Anything could happen; that's what happens with games. Someone will win and someone will lose or there will be a draw. Either way, it's a chance, and you don't like chances."

"Nick, you know how I used to feel about Victor, and you know how he hurt me. And . . ." She willed herself to go on. "You now know that he's Kam's father."

"I wasn't going to bring that up at this point. Even with that factor, and even though he hurt you, Fantasy, why play this game? Why did you even send the poor man a message? He would have gotten his in the end. How and when would have been for the Big Guy to decide, not you. And, as much as I will go to blows for you, it's not even for me to decide. You've got this thing all twisted."

"He needs to know my pain. All that I suffered and endured because he walked out without so much as a good-bye, he should suffer because of that." She jumped up, stood in front of Nick, and crossed her arms as if in a dare.

"Maybe, and maybe not. You never gave him the benefit of your anger. You faded into the backdrop and made it easy for the man to move on."

Fantasy thought about what Nick was saying. All of it was true. Now, she was having second thoughts. "So why, oh smart one, didn't you tell me this when I shared my brilliant plan with you in the beginning?"

"Oh, because I'm down for whatever and I'll support you to the end, right or wrong. But when I put two and two together and came up with Kam, it's just time to point out the wrong and to release you from walking around with this grudge. The real is you still love him, Fantasy. You never stopped loving him. Not to mention that you two share a child. You can't control what will happen between you, and while you are determined to stick to the plan and allow it to happen scene by scene, there is something about the best laid plans not working." Nick wondered for a second if he had correctly repeated the saying. "Things will turn out the way they are supposed to, regardless of what you do."

She thought about all he'd said, looked around her room, and felt defeated and better at the same time. Fantasy was a grown woman, definitely past the age of playing games, but hurt feelings mixed with love will make you do some crazy things. Whoever said it's a thin line between love and hate was right on the money. "I got it, and I hear you loud and clear." Fantasy dropped her hands to the side, seemingly defeated. "Let go and let God."

"Precisely." Nick applauded her. "Now, please do something to your hair and get the rest of your stuff together. You are monopolizing my time. I got places to go, people to see, and things to do."

"Oh, I'm sorry, Dee called right before you walked in and asked me to remind you to stop by the market and pick up some milk." Fantasy got up and walked to her suitcase without even looking in his direction. "You may not have heard your phone over your stereo system." She started laughing. Dee had her best friend on lock, and he was easily settling into a boyfriend-girlfriend routine. The message she had passed on was a to-do list, and those only existed between real couples.

"Whatever. I ain't got to get no milk. I was thinking about balling with the fellows for a few hours. Then, who knows? We may go for some drinks, have dinner, and hang out at the club. Who knows? The world is mine." He spread his arms out as if embracing invisible air.

"That may be, but somewhere in between your busy scheduled plans, you may want to pick up some milk." Fantasy laughed as she combed her loose curls and allowed them to cascade past her neckline. "I'm just saying there is no need to mess up your happy almost home behind not picking up some milk."

The plane ride to Florida hadn't been long and it wasn't bad at all. By the time she touched down, got through security, picked up her bags, and jumped on the shuttle, she was a little tired. The ride to the hotel was crowded and bumpy. When she reached her destination she was eager to get off, and she would rethink the shuttle route the next time real carefully. Fantasy was sure that a cab ride would have been so much better.

Fantasy yawned as she pulled her carry-on through the door, and the bellman followed with her other luggage. She stopped once she was in the living area of the suite, and placed the bag down. Reaching into her open drawstring bag, she pulled out a bill and handed it to him. "Thanks so much. I appreciate your assistance."

"No problem." He took another glance at Fantasy and noticed how shapely she was.

She saw him watching her and was flattered. She still had it and it was obviously in all the right places. He was a young-looking guy, and this bellman job was likely summer employment. He did a good enough job, but he didn't act as if this was his bread and butter, or that anyone other than himself relied on this income.

Before she gave way to complete exhaustion and sat down to rest, she decided to take the time to unpack and hang her things to get rid of some of the wrinkles. Once the task of unpacking was done, she went over to open the curtains a little more. The view from her hotel room was nice and it overlooked the pool. Her mind went back to her conversation with Nick. Fantasy sat down in the windowsill and gazed at the clouds. She had been switching among a few emotional states since Victor stepped back in. She didn't want to give him that much credit at all. It was the way it had been then, but she was young and now she had age and wisdom on her side, not to mention a hard-knock life with his initials on it. Her cell phone rang, disturbing her taking in the view and, most of all, her thoughts. She touched the screen and said, "Hello."

A woman confirmed who she was calling.

"Yes, this is Jordan Alexander."

"Ms. Alexander, I'm Senator Bell's assistant and I'm calling the press to let them know that the press conference has been moved up to five P.M. The senator had a conflicting meeting and six o'clock wouldn't do. I do his schedule all the time, and I don't know who in this office put something down without checking with me."

The lady had a serious Southern drawl. Fantasy looked puzzled. While the assistant was trying to figure out who had added something to the calendar, she was trying to figure out why she was sharing all this with her. "No problem, I'll be there. Thanks so much." Before she could receive some other information that was not her business, she touched the screen to end the call. There would be no time for a nap. Instead, she decided to take a shower, hoping that she would be totally revived and ready to take in the press conference. She'd be there earlier than the others, and if there were any juicy tidbits to be gathered that could remotely be newsworthy, she'd catch them. Fantasy turned on the flat-screen television and flipped to CNN. She reached into one of her bags and removed an oil warmer and two bottles of fragrant oils. Looking at the two bottles, she decided on Yankee vanilla and lime oil. After a few minutes, she had lit the tea candle and added a little water to the warmer, and the scent began to filter through the room. It was perhaps an extreme extra but she loved indulging in delicious smells, and it was a pampering thing that she loved. There were many others, and Nick and Kam had dubbed them all over-the-top. She didn't care. They were men. She was a girly girl and for her it was all necessary.

Fantasy had purposed in her mind to be on time. When she stepped out of the shower and took care of oiling, putting lotion on, spraying her body, and slipping on her Victoria's Secret bra and panties, she stood in front of the closet and slid the hangers. She had removed the white linen slacks, and she was just looking for the black silk wrap blouse. When she couldn't find it, she looked through the drawers and double checked to see if she had left something in the suitcase. The search took too much time, and she ended up wearing a navy print kimono dress and silver Nine West sandals. Her jewelry selection became another challenge before she picked simple diamond accessories.

Now she stood at the door of the meeting room where the press conference would take place, and noticed that the room was already filling up with news affiliates and the like. She could kick herself. Fantasy hadn't gotten the jump on a soul; they had, though, gotten the jump on her. She decided to get something to drink at one of the nearby refreshment tables. Both walls to the entrance of the room were lined with tables of finger foods, desserts, and drinks. She picked up a small bottle of grape juice and reached for a paper cup.

"Hello, Jordan," a voice from behind said.

She turned around and attempted a weak smile of recognition. "Hello, Anthony."

"It's been a very long time. But, as always, it's good to see you." He stood closer than he really needed to, but he wanted to make sure Fantasy was totally aware of his presence.

It was true; he hadn't seen her in a while, not since she'd ended their relationship. The two had the common interest of working in the syndicated news business, and, while it was a large arena, not many black females or males were on the fast track. He admired that about Jordan. She was excellent at what she did.

However, his efforts at making her a part of his future didn't work out. Jordan had told him that she just wasn't ready and there was too much else for her to focus on at that stage in her career. No other explanation was given, and after his continued calls went unanswered and the just-because gifts received no thank you, he gave up.

"It's good to see you too." Fantasy smiled slightly. He did look good, but he always looked good. Anthony Ortiz was a very attractive man and impeccably dressed all the time. He was a little on the light side and his Latino heritage was visible in his hair and complexion. They had been an item for more than a year.

"So how is Kameron?" Anthony asked. He and Kam had hit it off because they both loved sports, and he'd shown interest in any and everything that Kam talked about.

He had been the only man who'd made it into her inner family circle. Well, at least the circle that included one of her family members; he never made it to the level that included her grandparents. No one had. They knew she dated and that she had no preferences that would keep her from dating men. She just didn't feel they needed to be exposed to someone who wasn't going to be around for long.

"Kameron is great. He's in DC for an internship."

"Oh, great. Does he have the same cell number? I'm in DC next week. I'd love to call and see if he can swing hanging out with an old man." Anthony laughed, and his eyes seemed to laugh too.

"Yes, it's the same." Fantasy watched from out of the corner of her eye the hustle of people moving into the room, and knew it was time to go in. "Well, so much for a drink." She placed the juice back in the cooler.

"I'm sorry." He looked down, apologetic. "Tell you what. Why don't I take you to dinner after the press conference? It's the least I can do since I was so busy chatting, you didn't get a chance to even open the drink."

"That's okay. I'll get something later. I'm a little exhausted and need to rest." She was tired but not to the extent that it showed on her face. She didn't want to be alone in her own company, but boredom wasn't a good enough reason to consider Anthony's dinner invitation. He would have more questions than she wanted to answer, and the conversation would likely lead to what happened to them. And maybe there would even be an encore of "can we try again?" Life had been way too taxing lately for her to deal with any of that.

"I understand." He looked disappointed. Truthfully, he saw no harm in dinner. There were things he wanted to ask and a few things he wanted to say, but obviously she didn't want to hear any of it. He had always wondered what he had done wrong. It sort of made him fearful of launching out into the deep with the next woman. He decided not to push the envelope. "Well, tell you what, when the meeting is over I'll touch base with you. And keep in mind there is always tomorrow. I'm assuming you will be around for the continuation of all this fanfare?"

"Yes, I'll be around." She walked along with him and scanned the room for a seat. "I'll let you know." With that said, she walked near the front to the second row that had only one seat available. She crossed her fingers in hopes that the seat was not taken. Usually they were reserved for those on her level, but from where she stood she couldn't see what the sign at the end of the row said. Of course, Anthony was on the same level, but out of the corner of her eye she saw him head to the other side.

"Hello, is this seat available?" she questioned a lady who was hunched over some notes.

"Yes." She moved slightly so Fantasy could ease past her.

Just as she sat down, the left door opened and the senator's press team came out right before he did. She let out a breath. Not one minute to spare. She definitely had to work on her timing.

By the time she got back to the room it was almost 10:00. The press conference had gone well, even though she struggled to do what normally came as second nature to her. At times she was even bored. Fantasy had managed to raise her hand and ask a few questions that sounded intelligent to her and must have been perceived as appropriate for the senator, who answered each in great detail. She did get cornered by Anthony before she could exit the room, and she'd said, "Yes." In fact, she had already planned to agree as she sat there with questions and answers buzzing all around her head. She thought maybe spending some time with Anthony would kick her out of her funk, and fuel her to move out of the sandbox.

That's what she had thought. They walked a short distance to a quaint Italian restaurant, and made small talk.

"So tell me, how have things been going?" Anthony leisurely walked along the sidewalk, enjoying their walk to the nearby restaurant and the familiar scent of her perfume.

"Things have been going well. I have plenty of projects, and they're keeping me busy. But, then, that's nothing new." She walked beside her dinner escort, feeling the light breeze against her face. Fantasy looked up at the moonlight overhead and concentrated until she saw a few stars, she wished that she was in the company of someone that touched something deep on the inside. That special someone that stirred her romantic juices.

From what I remember, you live for busy." He opened the door to the restaurant and allowed Fantasy to enter.

The ambiance was very quaint and it created a subtle haven. There was a vintage aura, and a small band played in a room adjacent to the dining area. In the right company, all of what surrounded her could have been romantic. Romance was the very last thing on her mind. "Once upon a time. It seems that the excitement of it all isn't the same."

"I can relate. I've been feeling that way a lot too," said Anthony. "Must be something in the media circuit air."

They had only stood for a minute or two when they were greeted by a young man. "Welcome to Patelli's. Will it just be two for dinner?"

Anthony responded, "Yes."

"Very well. Follow me." He seated them at a small table near the center of the room. It was covered by a red and white tablecloth. At the center of the table there were fresh, colorful flowers arranged in a tulip bud vase. It added a nice touch. "Have you been to Patelli's before?" he questioned.

Again, Anthony spoke for both of them. "No, we haven't."

Just then Fantasy remembered at least one thing that slightly irritated her about Anthony. He had this way of taking the lead. She glanced at the host as he talked and smiled, hoping he realized that she could speak for herself.

"Well, welcome. You are in for a wonderful dining experience. The food here is authentic Italian, and quite superb. Not to mention the menu is very extensive." He smiled as he handed them their menus. "Please enjoy your dinner and the music." He nodded toward the band that continued to play.

Again Anthony spoke. "Thank you." He opened the menu, but hadn't bothered to take his eyes off Fantasy. "It is so nice to see you again."

She only glanced at him. There was no need to allow her vision to linger because she knew what she would see. "You said that already." She let out a nervous laugh.

"I know, but some things bear repeating." Anthony couldn't help but state the obvious. He had thought about her often, and yet he'd honored her decision to end things.

Almost before the server could put the crystal water glass down, Fantasy sipped the water that was placed in front of her. "Thank you."

"You're very welcome." A young lady—who looked Italian and who looked similar to the young man—waited on them. "My name is Renita and I'll be taking care of you tonight. If you like, I'll give you a little more time to look over the menu. While you do that, I'll bring out a basket of hot breadsticks." She smiled. "Did you want to put an appetizer in now?" She watched them both study the menu.

"Yes, please. I'll have calamari." Fantasy couldn't believe she'd actually beaten him in deciding on an appetizer.

Anthony looked at Fantasy. "That sounds good. Do you mind sharing?"

"No, not at all," Fantasy said.

Once Renita walked toward the rear of the restaurant and through a door, Fantasy decided to make small talk. She was hoping it would avoid the one conversation she didn't want to have. "How is your mother?"

"Very well. She's as busy as ever and doesn't want to slow down. I try not to interrupt what seems to keep her going." He relaxed a little more and took a sip of the cold water.

"Please tell her that I asked about her." She had met his mother on a few occasions. From the very first visit she'd welcomed Fantasy into her home.

"I will do that."

"So what assignments have you taken on lately?" Fantasy quizzed, feeling confident that this wouldn't be a one- or two-word answer.

Anthony began to share, and, just as she'd thought, it became a detailed conversation. They shared the profession, so she was anything but bored. The appetizer came and dinner was ordered as Anthony continued to share.

The two old friends continued, and soon they were laughing and joking like old times. Fantasy was really enjoying his company. She had almost forgotten how much fun he was.

All went well until the dessert came.

"Do you remember the first dessert we shared?" Anthony picked up his fork and cut a small portion of the Italian cream cake.

Her forehead suddenly felt warm. She should have known better than to think that none of this would lead back down memory lane. "Not exactly." She was trying not to sound irritated. Of course she remembered. Remembering things was part of her profession.

He knew that she did, but he went ahead and spoke. "It was Godiva cheesecake. I've been in love with that stuff ever since."

She smiled and focused on the dessert. It was one of her favorites, but only because cheesecake had always been. And it had been the get-over-whatever-ails-you dessert in college. She and Victor had shared cheesecake on so many evenings. "If you don't mind, I'm going to call it an evening," Fantasy said.

The short walk back to the hotel was silent for the most part. Their good night was even shorter, with Fantasy reaching out to shake his hand instead of yielding to the embrace he attempted to give. "Thank you so much for dinner and great company."

"I'll be in touch." He wanted so much more and yet he felt shut out. He'd call as he'd said he would.

It ended like that. She paced the suite the minute the door closed and her purse hit the chair cushion. Needing to do something, she dialed Kameron and got his voice mail. She quickly left a message and went on to dial Nick.

"Hello," Dee answered Nick's phone.

"Oh, hey, Dee. I was calling for Nick, but if you two are busy he can call me later," she said.

"Oh no. Here he is. Believe it or not, he's cooking me dinner. Here, sweetheart, it's Fantasy."

Nick answered, "Hey, girl. What's going on? How was the senator's press conference? Did he make the big announcement, or is he baiting you guys until tomorrow?"

"Tomorrow. Listen, I didn't want to interrupt you. But did Dee say you were cooking? I thought you said that would be something you'd never do for a love interest." She chuckled. Nick was bending rules left and right.

"I know, rub it in later." He laughed with his friend, but sensed she had something on her mind. "Listen, I can have Dee watch the food and we can chat if you need to."

"We can talk tomorrow. Go on and cook." Fantasy tried to move toward upbeat. "You like her and that's good."

Nick paused and thought about what Fantasy was saying. "Yeah, I do. Call me tomorrow." He was about to hang up, and added, "I love you."

"I love you too, Nick." Fantasy hung up and immediately dialed again. This would be the last call and she would go to bed, hopefully feeling something other than what she felt.

"Hello." Her nana answered sounding out of breath.

"Hello, Nana; are you okay?" Fantasy moved to the edge of the sofa, all ready to pack up and go home if need be.

"Oh, Fantasy. Child, I'm sorry. Just a little out of breath." She coughed to clear her throat, but offered nothing else.

Fantasy heard her grandfather call out for her grandmother in the background. He was telling her to come back and get some more good loving. That was the confirmation she needed. Her grandfather was indeed taking the blue pills, and judging from how they had been acting lately, he was hitting the bottle on a regular basis.

"You know what, Nana, you go on in there with Granddad. I'll call you guys later."

"Okay, baby. Well, you are all right, aren't you?" Pearl asked.

This was not her nana. Her nana would have stopped everything to talk to her grandchild. "I'm fine, Nana, and I love you."

"I love you too, sweetness." She hung up the phone without even saying good-bye.

Fantasy laughed until tears came to her eyes. She couldn't believe them. There was no one else to call but Victor, and instead of calling, she went to the computer and opened the application to send an e-mail.

Hi. I hope all is well with you. I was just thinking about you and wondering how you are and what you are doing. It's funny; just as my day is ending your day is about to begin. A day with endless possibilities, and one to be embraced. I can't really explain myself or my actions lately. A friend said that it had something to do with discovering an old friend on Facebook. Maybe that's what it is. Whatever it is, I hope I'm not alone. Good night, Victor. Fantasy

Fantasy turned off the computer and got ready for bed. As she climbed in, she reached to turn off the nearby light on the nightstand. One of the things that she realized most of all, and especially after tonight, was that she was lonely. Not just for anyone; if she had wanted, Anthony would have spent more time with her. Fantasy knew she was lonely for Victor. She nervously touched her lips, thinking about how soft his kisses used to be. Next week she would come face-to-face with him, and, after all this time, she would kiss him again. She would not be in control, and, despite how she wanted to play the game, that was okay with her.

Nick was right, she was not in control. Despite what she thought would happen, she wasn't sure if things would play out that way. The fact was that she was beginning to have second thoughts.

Chapter 12

"Chief Charles, I'm sorry to tell you this, but the test results show that one of your kidneys is not functioning properly." He slipped his glasses from his white coat and put them on. Opening the file before him, he continued. "This would explain almost all of the symptoms you are having."

Victor sat in front of the desk and couldn't move. He heard the words that were coming out of the doctor's mouth and he understood each one of them. Already in his mind he was saying it over and over again: kidney disease. "Are you sure?"

"Yes. I even had them run the tests twice. I wanted to have an accurate diagnosis." He opened another folder, and continued. "I can tell you all about it and what we need to do to get a handle on your medical situation."

"You don't have to tell me all about it. My dad dealt with kidney disease for a long time before he died." Just saying that made his prognosis seem very dim.

"Well, I don't know how long your father has been dead, or if he died from kidney failure. But there have been so many great advances and successes in dealing with the disease. With the right transplant, you could live a very normal, healthy life."

He simply nodded. "So what comes before that step, dialysis?" He asked the question he already knew the answer to.

"We will begin that right away and get your system back doing what it is supposed to do. You may want to take some time away from your duties for a while."

"Listen, I'm away from my daughter and away from home. I know there is no right time to be ill and no right time to face a disease that requires time, treatment, and the right match. However, I'd like to go home first, and when I return, we can start treatment. I don't think ten days will make a difference. If I need to start sooner, then you can arrange that with the hospital there. I'll be in DC and can go to Walter Reed to start treatment."

"Well, I'd really like for you to start right away. Just call the office and let me know when you are leaving, and I will arrange the treatment to begin once you are there a few days and settled enough to go in. Why don't you consider staying there for a thirty-day period? The transition of coming back here after only ten days may be too much."

"Well, let me think about it. It does sound like it may work out better. I'll have to talk to the general, and I'll get back with your office tomorrow." Victor didn't think he'd be able to get it done by the end of the day. Tomorrow would have to do. And it was his decision, so the doctor would just have to go with it.

"Okay. Keep in mind that people do live well once they go through the necessary steps and take good care of themselves. We go into this with a great advantage because you are in excellent health."

"I'll be in touch." Victor reached to shake the doctor's hand and turned to leave.

He didn't hear the receptionist as she said good-bye. He passed right by one of the guys he always talked to at church. His thoughts were consuming him. How was he going to tell his mother he was sick? He made a point of talking to her every Sunday. It had been that way ever since he went into the Air Force. He would need time to find the words to tell her he was sick with the very thing that killed his father. Then there was Niya, who he wanted to see married and with children. There was so much life left for him to live. He couldn't, even for a second, see this as an end. Just as he got into the car, he dropped the keys out of his trembling hands and onto the floor.

He spoke out loud, "Fantasy." The door for them was open and he was elated to walk through and receive, so far, something that seemed so promising. Victor believed that there was a chance for the future. Her last message had said as much. She wanted them to be on the same page and he believed with all his heart and soul that they were. If anything, he was a few chapters ahead of her. Victor wiped at the tear that escaped. He was a man in every sense of the word, even though some would assume that real men don't cry. He just didn't think holding back any emotion, especially tears would make him less of a man. He'd fight this and do all he could. There was no way he would be cheated twice. There was no way he'd disappoint her or leave her again. Not even in death, if he could help it.

The first thing he'd do would be to tell the general and ask for leave to take the necessary steps to get better. Then, he'd change his flight and get started on the treatment. He would still go to the meeting but, most of all, he'd be in place when Fantasy came to meet him. From there he really wasn't sure what the next step would be. He just hoped that, as much as possible, he wouldn't have to make it alone. His dad had always reminded him to be strong. He took that to heart and displayed as much as possible a strong front. Victor even had a Chinese symbol tattooed on his arm with the words "be strong." This was the eye of the storm, but he was determined to come out of it and not allow it to consume him. There was too much to live for.

One of his young airmen would always say, "Live life, don't let life live you." He never paid the saying Bobby would recount any mind until this very moment. The young man's life had ended way too soon by senseless violence. He was a good kid, and Victor always believed he was in heaven, smiling down, reminding those he loved to live life. Today he felt that more than ever.

"Man, I can't believe the game ended like that." Darryl picked up his can of soda from a coaster.

"It is what it is. If I were a betting man, I would have your money right about now. Didn't nobody tell you to put all your stock in the Mariners tonight? They're not even your main team."

"Anybody is my team when they playing against the Orioles," Darryl replied. The two had been relaxing and enjoying the game. He wanted to hang out with Victor before he left on TDY. Darryl also noticed when he saw him earlier in the day that he seemed a little heavy. If Victor needed to share, he wanted to be there for him.

"That's why you looking like someone took your candy. Boy, you better get with the Orioles and stop playing. Those guys are playing ball." Victor tried to stay upbeat. He had taken care of everything that needed his attention and tied up all the loose ends. The situation with Lopez was even taken care of and she had been reassigned. Donovan, a male, would be his new assistant. He didn't have to disclose exactly what had happened, which he felt spared her reputation and kept her from turning the tables on him. All he knew was that they'd accepted what he had to say and removed her.

"Whatever, I thought you was my boy for life. I'll give them a thumbs up today and maybe a few stars, but they ain't all that."

"I am your boy. Just give credit where credit is due." Victor laughed. He decided to go ahead and tell Darryl. It was getting late and he would have to get up at 3:00 to make it to the airport in time for his flight. He sat back in his recliner and sipped his ginger ale. "You know life will throw you a curve ball."

"It threw you one and you are working overtime to catch it. Not to mention long distance. That is, if I haven't missed anything in the last forty-eight hours. You are still having your Facebook affair, aren't you?" Darryl asked.

"I am. We have even incorporated a daily phone conversation. The best part is that she will be meeting me in DC." Victor felt good about saying that. There were relationships that blossomed solely from e-mailing, dating sites, and probably even Facebook. He wasn't sure that he and Fantasy fell into that category since they already knew each other.

"Well, go ahead with your bad self," Darryl said.

"But, on a serious note, I went to the doctor the other day to check out the nausea and the exhaustion. You know I mentioned that I've been feeling like something ran over me for at least a month or so."

Darryl nodded that he remembered.

"Anyway, I got the results back two days ago and they discovered that one of my kidneys is malfunctioning."

Darryl moved to the edge of his chair. “What?” He looked at Victor really hard. Of course, there were no gigantic signs that would display what was going on inside his friend’s body.

“That’s what the test showed.” Victor continued to try to be upbeat. His emotions had gone all over the place and back. He was feeling a little too in touch with his sensitive side. There were times when he would watch an emotional show or movie and end up in tears.

The first time Fantasy had witnessed his tears was during some movie; he couldn’t remember what it was. She didn’t laugh at him, but held his hand and told him it was okay. That was in the heat of the moment. The very next day she told him they would limit the sad movies and do drama and action-packed films. They had both laughed it off.

“Well, do they need to retest you? Lots of times they have people all in a panic, and when they retest them nothing is there.” Darryl was grasping at straws, but he didn’t want to accept the diagnosis any more than he was sure his friend did.

“He had them test twice. The results are accurate.” Victor paused. “Come on, man, don’t be all down in the mouth. I’m going to go ahead and take an extended leave and handle this in the States. They will do what they need to do and if it comes down to it then they will find me a kidney. I’ll be as good as new and ready to get you out on the court in no time.”

“I hear you. Don’t think just because you on the injury list that I’m going to take pity on you.” Darryl’s laughter didn’t cover up his worry. “You know that if you need anything, including a kidney, let me know.”

“You are crazy.”

"No, seriously. I will see if I'm a match. I know you have Niya and maybe some other relatives down the line. But if God brought us together as brothers, it may be for a reason." Darryl felt himself choking up.

"Well, that's good to know. I'll be talking to you, and if my back gets against the wall I may just take you up on that." Victor stood up, and so did Darryl. They looked at each other for a few seconds and then the two embraced. "Go ahead and get out of here and see what you can get into. It's still early for you. I'm going to hit the bed. Three o'clock will be here before I know it. In a few days I'll be with Fantasy and I must say, man, I'm looking forward to it."

"I'm sure you are. Stay strong." Darryl pounded his fist against Victor's. "It's already done, man. Don't sweat this." He opened the door and left.

Victor knew exactly what he was telling him. Darryl did a lot of things that he wasn't proud of, but he was a religious man. He believed that everything that happened should be committed to prayer. Darryl wasn't the only one praying. Victor had been sending them up ever since he'd gotten the news. Some waited until bad things happened before they bent down on their knees and prayed, but Victor was grateful that he not only prayed when there was a problem, he prayed when all was well. He was no stranger to the faith and works things, and he was thankful that he and God were on a first-name basis.

Chapter 13

Ever since she touched down from shiny Florida, Fantasy had gone into overdrive to stay on top of things. In two days she had managed to get more done than she had in a few months. Not because she had stopped thinking about Victor, but because she just accepted that she couldn't control her feelings. There was something to be said about relinquishing power. A heart will feel what it wants to feel and do what it wants to do. Fantasy had heard that somewhere along her travels and it was so true. She gave up mapping out her life to the letter, and as for Victor Charles, she'd just see what way the wind would blow. She thought out loud. "The unseen wind moves the sail." Normally when she recalled what Valerie Whitman would say, it always had something to do with having the upper hand and knowing how to take control: a lesson she'd learned too well. The thing about the wind being unseen summed it all up. Whatever happened would take on its own life. It would be moved by something much deeper than them, something beyond the control of either of them. Fantasy was positive that it would move.

The office phone rang and she frowned because she was officially off. She started not to answer it, but thought it might be important. "Jordan Alexander."

"Hello, Jordan. I just thought I'd give you a call to see if you made it back to Charlotte safely." Anthony's strong voice spoke through the phone.

"Hello, Anthony." What was he thinking? She was up and down the coast—and all over the globe, for that matter—and he was calling to check on her after a flight that barely got up in the air? "I made it back in one piece."

"I was just thinking about you. As I mentioned, I'll be in DC next week, and I still plan to call Kameron to see if he wants to hang out."

She threw her head back and rolled her eyes around. Next week, Fantasy thought. She would still be in DC next week. She didn't think about that when he'd mentioned visiting Kam when she saw him. It was a big city and chances were likely that their paths would never cross. Since there was a small chance that she could bump into him, or Kam, for that matter, she was planning to stay low key.

Fantasy had no plans of even telling Kam that she would be in the area. The last thing she needed was for him and Victor to end up seeing each other. She was all for sightseeing, and had already listed a few places she wanted to go, but she thought she might need to scale back her list. Then again, she could travel during peak vacationer times with the hopes of blending in. She would also need to remember all the restaurants and nightspots she had gone to with Anthony and avoid them.

"Oh, by all means, call him. I forgot to mention to him that I had seen you." She hadn't forgotten; it was not important enough to mention. If she was lucky, Kam would be too busy to see him. There was also a chance that going to dinner or hanging out with Anthony wouldn't be high on his must-do list.

"I can't wait to see him." Anthony rambled on about the time they went to see the Bobcats play and the time the three of them went to Disney World.

She listened for as long as she could and finally she just interrupted him. "Anthony, I've really got to run. I'm on the road again tomorrow and I haven't finished packing." That was a stretch of the truth. Not wanting to get caught up like she did last time, she was already packed and everything was neatly in place by the door. The only two things she hadn't done, which were intentionally left for last, were get her hair done and make a visit to her favorite spa. Fantasy had made late appointments for both. She hoped the spa visit would have her relaxed enough to sleep through the night, instead of bouncing up every few minutes with nervous energy. She was hoping her hair would still look good in the morning, even if she had to sleep with her hands under her chin. She giggled to herself. That was something she hadn't done in years, not since she was young and cared what some guy or guys thought of how she looked.

"Oh, I understand completely." Anthony was hoping the next question wouldn't meet cold opposition. There had to be something there for old time's sake. At one point early on they had been good together. There was no one who could tell him that he and Fantasy hadn't shared something special. He'd felt it, and he had never stopped feeling it. Anthony just hoped that maybe she felt it too.

"Well, maybe when I get back from DC I can come see you. Or, if it's more convenient, you can come visit me. Either way, Fantasy, I'd love to see you."

She didn't want to hurt his feelings. Fantasy sensed the sensitivity that had slipped in as they were talking. "I'll tell you what, I'll call you the minute I get back."

"That would be great." His voice held an upbeat, hopeful tone. "Have a safe trip, and I look forward to talking to you."

By the time she hung up the phone and glanced at her watch, she noticed that it was time to make her way for her early evening pampering. Fantasy stood up and took a look in the mirror. She ran her fingers through her hair and pulled it up on top of her head. She turned her head from side to side and tried to imagine another look. She wanted to do something drastic; something really different. Victor hadn't seen her in two decades, other than the headshots on the Facebook site. She didn't consider either of them great photos. Oh well. She let her hair down. Considering a hair change was a thought, she decided to call Tee on the way to the salon so she could come up with a few possibilities. Tee was the same age as her son and she absolutely adored her. She had been her stylist for three years. This was after Vicki, her previous hair wiz, relocated to Atlanta. All of Vicki's clients at Endeavors were moving over to the girls who had been there forever, while Fantasy decided to put her hair in the hands of Tee, who had just acquired a chair and used to shampoo her hair for Vicki. The union of hair stylist and client was ideal, and they became close as could be.

"I can't believe you are giving me a creative green light." Tee giggled as she combed and snipped Fantasy's hair. She wore her customary black Endeavors smock. Her hair was done in microbraids, and she had them pulled up and held in place by a black elastic band. A few braids were loosely hanging down past her neck.

"Just don't get carried away. You've been cutting like a mad woman." Fantasy couldn't help but notice her hair on the floor all around the chair. It had been awhile since she had gone short, and then it had not been super short. The maintenance of short hair was something she didn't have time for.

"I got this," Tee said.

During the next hour, Fantasy got her hair cut, relaxed, washed, conditioned, and roller set. Normally she was very patient, but this evening she was ready to finish with the hair and get the spa visit out of the way. Really, having them both done would put her closer to boarding the flight to DC and seeing Victor again. He had asked countless times for her to join him for a Skype video conversation. Each time she'd declined, wanting to wait for their in-person encounter.

"Oh, mom. I've outdone myself." Tee's eye lit up when she looked at Fantasy. Fantasy closed her eyes tight before seeing what they had talked each other into.

"Oh my God, Tee. Look at it. Nana's going to have a fit. She thinks a woman's hair is her crowning glory and mine is all over the floor."

"Well, there's not much we can do about it now. Besides, it's a little late in the evening for me to weave some in." Tee laughed and took the smock off of Fantasy. "I like it, and Nana will too. Not to mention the hint of color is popping."

"Okay, Tee, talk my language." Fantasy pulled at one of the curls and it coiled right back up. Tee had cut her hair to a short crop, created carefree spiral curls all over, and highlighted some strands with a rich mocha hue. It was, in Fantasy's opinion, to die for, and she hoped her hair alone was enough to knock him to his knees.

"Popping like fireworks, mom." Tee lightly touched Fantasy's shoulder, and smiled.

Tee adored Fantasy. She had done so much for her. Fantasy had helped her get her own place so she could move out of the place she had shared with a trifling, no-account boyfriend. She had also helped put her son in private school. In short, she owed her a lot. She was more of a mother than her own mother had been. From the beginning, she'd started calling Fantasy "Mom" and she never objected, and neither did Kam, who considered Tee an adopted sister.

"Well, let's hope he thinks so." She turned around.

"Mom, let's do your eyebrows real quick, and then you can head over to the spa area."

"Great. Oh, before I forget, ask Troy to decide whether he wants a gift card or if he would prefer that I take him to start his Christmas shopping."

"I'm sure he would prefer you to go with him. I took him this weekend to pick up a few things, and he had no problem telling me that his grandma Fantasy was doing the rest." Tee smiled. "I'd like to think he was just looking out for my wallet, but I really think he'd prefer you. I swear he is five going on fifty-five."

"Leave my little man alone. I'll call you when I get back." Fantasy stood up, and looked at her eyebrows and then her hair. "You did a great job."

"No problem, Mom. And please tell me all about this mystery man when you return. I can't believe I know something that Kam doesn't know for once." Tee had had a crush on Kam in the beginning, but she'd never approached him, since she felt more like his sister. She didn't want to mess up a good thing or great friendships.

"Here." Fantasy hugged Tee and placed some money in her pocket. "I'll talk to you soon."

"Okay." She didn't have to look in her pocket to know that it was much more than what was needed to cover the service she'd provided. It always was. She lived for the day that she could give it back or tell Fantasy not to worry about it. For now, she needed all the extra she could get. Being a single mother was hard work.

By the time Fantasy left Endeavors she looked good and she felt wonderful. Wow, she thought. Her cell phone rang five times before she could locate it in the bottom of her bag. She answered just in time. "Hello."

"Hello there. And how was your evening of beauty?" Victor's voice came through the phone.

She didn't know if it was in her mind or if he really sounded closer since he was now in the States instead of in Germany.

"It was great. I'm totally relaxed." Fantasy had allowed her guard to fall a little, and her plan had been adjusted to the status of just seeing what would happen.

"I can't wait to see you. I went out and got an African American haircut." He had joked with Fantasy about how difficult it was to get a decent haircut in Germany. None of the barbers were black and his hair had suffered many bad haircuts because of it. "I even went out today and did a little shopping for both of us."

"And what did you get me this time?" Fantasy smiled. Every week since they had been talking there was always a delivery. Once she'd told him that she collected Thomas Blackshear figurines and reported exactly what she owned, she had received a collectible every other week. On the off weeks he was adding to her clown and mask collection. He joked at first about her obsession with clowns, but once she explained that they were happy regardless, he understood and decided to indulge her.

"If I told you, Fantasy, it wouldn't be a surprise, now, would it?" He chuckled.

"I guess it wouldn't." Fantasy was still parked in the lot near the salon. "Hold on a second and let me put my earpiece in. Then I can drive home."

"Oh, okay. No problem."

After a second, Fantasy spoke. "Okay, I think I'm straight." She put her Cadillac SRX into drive and pulled off. "Well, two can play. While I was shopping, I picked up your birthday gift."

Victor was silent. He had not mentioned to Fantasy that tomorrow was his birthday. When he decided to attended the function in DC, he realized that the timing was perfect. And once he got her to consent to come, it was even better. For him, seeing her was the best birthday gift he could receive. "My birthday?"

"Yes, it's tomorrow. I won't say how old you will be." Fantasy smiled, knowing she had blown him away. She remembered his birthday every year. This year was no exception. The only difference was that she would be seeing him.

"I can't believe you remembered. It's not on Facebook." Victor wondered if he had mentioned it, but he knew he hadn't.

"No, it's not. Just accept that I know when your birthday is. And don't bother asking me what I picked up. You will see me and your gift tomorrow."

She turned into her gated community. It was beautiful, and just driving through the gate always made her feel so blessed. Fantasy had never struggled, not even as a child growing up. It was all because of what her mother did for a living.

After a while, Valerie no longer dealt with the regular clientele or put herself in the lineup. She ran things and her customer base included only a few, so few that Fantasy could count them on three fingers. Her grandparents already had. They didn't live as large as their daughter, but her grandfather had retired from the phone company and Pearl was a school teacher. Both occupations were legal and upstanding. Pearl and Matthew didn't want to take any money from their daughter, but when Valerie was killed she had left everything to them for the care of her daughter. A few months after her death, once Fantasy had settled in a bit and the nightmares weren't occurring every night, they received a certified package. In the package was a note from a man saying that he'd promised Val that if anything ever happened to her, he would provide for her daughter. There was a check for six figures, and the checks continued to show up in the mail until Fantasy was eighteen. All of the money, including what was left from Val, was put in an account. Some was used for college and graduate school. And Fantasy had used some to purchase the house and to buy a car for Kam, but other than that it was just earning interest. Her grandparents never spent any, nor would they ever accept anything. She had managed to renovate their house and purchase a new pickup truck for her granddad when he retired.

"Well, I can't wait. Does that mean I have to hang up now? You know I never want to hang up." Victor lay back against the pillows on the bed. He didn't mean for it to, but his anatomy was responding to her soft voice and just the thought of seeing her. He just hoped that he could control himself when he saw her up close and personal.

"You do have to hang up if you want me to get my beauty rest and be at my best tomorrow." Fantasy didn't want to hang up either. But there were a few more things to check before she retired for the evening. She was relieved that she'd be in the air for only an hour and fifteen minutes. If it was any longer than that she would come completely undone. She was as eager to see Victor as he was to see her.

"Well, I'll hang up for now. Just know that my voice will be the first voice you hear in the morning. I'm not even letting you sleep past six."

"Victor, you better not call me all early. My flight doesn't leave until noon and I'm not planning on getting up early." She had been sitting in her garage with the motor off, but was still talking. Sometimes he had her feeling like a teenager all over again. Only teenagers would talk endlessly, and with each new conversation they would have just as much to talk about as the last time, or sometimes nothing to talk about at all. They had done their share of just listening to one another breathe, even in their old age of knowing better. Even when she thought her tough-girl plan was working, it was breaking pitifully.

"I plan to and I will." Victor chuckled. "I can't imagine being able to sleep tonight. It's only fair you share the sleeplessness."

"How do you know you won't be able to sleep?" Fantasy asked.

"For one, my body has not adjusted to being in the States yet, and I'm talking to the other reason." He smiled; it was so true.

"If you must call, I'll answer." She giggled. Fantasy knew she wouldn't be able to sleep. Victor calling that early wouldn't be a problem.

"Well, sweetheart, I'll talk with you at six." Victor didn't want to, but he hung up the phone.

Fantasy got herself together and got out of her car. It was going to be a long night, or a long morning. Either way, she knew she wouldn't be sleeping that much. Her heart was full right now. It was better than the uneasy, crazy up-and-down stuff she had been feeling. She'd take this over that any day of the week. It felt good, but as she also knew it might end in a shipwreck. She inhaled as she placed her keys in their usual spot; the last thing she needed was to spend time looking for them tomorrow. As she walked down the hall to her bedroom and turned on the lights, she exhaled the breath she had inhaled and smiled. The room was soothing and she hoped it worked its wonders tonight. The massage was a good start and she was going to do whatever she could to keep her relaxed buzz going. Instead of turning on the television, she hit a button on the stereo remote and cued up disc three. She waited to hear the first chord, and when it came through the surround-sound speakers that were hidden around the room, she melted.

Luther Vandross filled the room and she thought about the first time she'd heard him live, the exact moment her favorite singer stood on the stage and began to sing this song. A group of them had gone to the show, and while they had not come together, Victor was among the posse. Somehow he'd ended up sitting right next to her. This was before his confession of being attracted to her, and well after she had noticed him and liked everything she saw. Throughout the night, she would steal glances of Victor and his expression as they were serenaded by song after song. He had been so into it. Sonya had had some family emergency, and Fantasy had him all to herself; at least, in her mind. She dared not do anything that would be out of place or alert some of Sonya's friends that she was after their girl's man. She kept a safe distance, but at one point she felt his arm against her arm and the feel of him made her quiver. He must have felt it because he asked if she was cold. She remembered answering that she was fine, and she tried hard to turn her attention back to Luther, but it was no use. Their eyes locked, and for a minute there was something. From that point on, whenever he looked at her she felt it, and she hoped that he felt it too. The first night in his apartment he'd played that song, and he told her that he felt what she felt that night. He looked at her the same way he had that night and she knew that what she saw was real.

Fantasy lay on the bed, dressed in a nightshirt. She forgot all about falling asleep on her hair. Before she knew it, she had fallen into a peaceful slumber, listening to their song on repeat.

Chapter 14

Victor was at Dulles Airport two hours before Fantasy's flight was due to land. He had been in DC for the past five days and had already met with a specialist at the Walter Reed Army Medical Center. At his request, Victor had repeated a few tests and done some additional testing. There were tests done that he understood and others that he couldn't see having any correlation to what was going on with him. He was assured that they were all necessary, and that everything together would give the doctors an expert view of his situation. Then they would know how much damage his kidneys had already sustained. They'd also know if any other organs were affected. With all that concluded, they would establish a plan of action.

He asked up front for a few uninterrupted days. He was given approval and reminded to take it easy. He would be taking it easy the minute Flight 2530 landed, with one passenger in particular making her way toward him.

Victor hadn't budged. Other than going to the bathroom, which was an absolute necessity, he would be planted right there in a seat facing the terminal she would be exiting. He looked at his watch a thousand times. Just as his legs were getting numb, he saw commotion coming from the gate and quickly stood up. He was dressed in jeans and a red polo. Considering the fact that he was always in uniform and military gear, this was a switch. He wasn't sure what to wear; a suit was too much, his uniform was too over the top, so he decided that cool and casual was the way to go. Victor nervously brushed from his pants invisible lint or whatever he thought he saw, and wondered if he should have worn the striped polo shirt. Not knowing what to do with his hands, he rubbed them over his short hair and then down his face. There was a light bead of sweat on his lip. If she didn't come through the gate soon, he just knew he would pass out.

Then, he saw her.

She was looking down into her bag. Even from a distance he knew it was Fantasy. From where he stood she looked good. Victor sat down, afraid that he would fall down. He breathed in and out slowly, and again he stood up.

Two tall guys the size of linebackers moved out of the way and she came into full view. Just then she stopped searching in her purse and looked up, and she saw him. He watched her intensely as a smile came over her face. It seemed so bright. They must have been thinking the same thing and on the same wavelength, because she was dressed in jeans and a blouse.

Victor felt a tear and reached to wipe it away before she got closer. He even turned his back and wiped it real good, hoping it would stop by the time he turned back around.

He tried to wait for her to get to him but it didn't seem to be happening fast enough. With his eyes still fixed on Fantasy, Victor started walking toward her.

It was if no one else was in the airport. He navigated through the crowd, which wasn't an easy task because the place was packed and as busy as ever.

Finally, when the distance between them closed and they stood directly in front of one another, Victor looked at her and grinned so wide his face felt like it would crack at the corners. He reached for both of her elbows and looked down at her. "Fantasy, I can't believe I'm looking at you. It's so good to see you."

"It's great to see you, Victor. You haven't changed at all," she said.

"You haven't cither. But you look more beautiful than you did before, if that's possible." Hoping it wasn't too forward, he bent down and lightly kissed her cheek.

Fantasy closed her eyes the minute he came toward her. She didn't think that he was going to kiss on the mouth, but she knew that his soft lips were going to brush against some part of her face. He smelled so good and the scent of him enveloped her. "Thank you for the wonderful compliment, and happy birthday. You don't look a day over . . ." She stopped, put her finger over her lips, and looked up, as if she was trying to rcmember.

"The jokes start, huh?" He laughed. She could always make him laugh. "Thank you." He beamed, still impressed that she remembered. Victor had moved his hands from her elbows to her hands, and he just held on with the same big grin on his face.

For the first few minutes, she didn't say anything, and then she spoke. "Victor, you are still so goofy. Let go of my hands and let's go get my bags. I don't think you want our visit to be spent here in the middle of the airport." She removed her hands and pulled the tote farther up on her arm.

"You're right." He was still smiling. "Here, let me get that for you." He reached for her tote and held it in his hand. As if by impulse, he placed his hand on the small of her back, and the two headed toward the baggage claim area. "Before we start our visit, can I say one thing?" They had walked only a few steps, and he stopped and looked down at her.

Fantasy was thinking as they walked together that he'd seemed so much taller then. But then she was much shorter. He still towered over her, but only slightly. "What do you want to say, Victor?" She was so totally amused with him. He had always showered her with attention, and, being with him only for a few minutes, she could see that trait had not changed.

He put the tote down and pulled her into his arms. "It's not so much what I want to say as it is what I want to do." His lips touched hers and she tasted so good. He couldn't believe the feeling that flowed through him. The bonus was that she kissed as well as she always had.

Fantasy received his warm kiss and kissed him back. They shared the same kiss and it ignited the same feelings. It was a totally clean kiss and yet it held so much passion. When he removed his lips from hers, she cleared her throat. "Well, thank you for telling me that." She looked around quickly and noticed that a few people looked at them as if they should get a room. There were also a few others who smiled, likely thinking that they were a couple who had not seen each other for a very long time.

"I am so glad that you are here with me." Victor was sincere in what he said. He realized that Fantasy could have easily said no, or somewhere in the days that followed her yes, she could have changed her mind. The truth was that Fantasy could have walked away and never opened the door. But none of that had happened. And she was standing there in front of him.

"Now we can go." Victor picked the tote back up and they were on their way.

They navigated their way out of the airport and made their way to where the rental car was parked. Victor put all the suitcases in the trunk and clicked the doors open. Before she could even reach for the doorknob, he was there beside her, opening the door.

"Thanks." She got in and placed her purse on the floor. She wanted to pull the mirror down just to see what he was seeing, especially since she had not had time to go to the restroom and freshen up. Hopefully she didn't look that bad. The flight had not been that long. She did reach into her purse and pull out a stick of gum, and quickly placed it in her mouth.

Victor got in the car and put the key in the ignition. "You're breath is okay. At least, it was when I kissed you a few minutes ago. Should I check it again?"

She laughed. Fantasy was glad that his sense of humor was still in full effect. "No, thank you. What you can do is feed me. Do you think you can handle that?" She looked around to see if there was some place close by, but of course all she could see around her was the spacious parking lot.

"Of course I can handle that." Victor had figured she would be hungry. Being adamant about preparation, he already had a few places in mind. "My meetings are in DC, so I thought we could stay in the Tyson's Corner area and just go wherever from there. I didn't think you wanted to be in the heart of DC." He paused. "I mean, I hope that's okay. I didn't even ask before I made arrangements." He had started stumbling over his words as if he had just made a mistake or major error.

Fantasy touched his hand that was positioned over the gearshift. "Victor, that's fine. I never asked because you told me to allow you to take care of it. I was just allowing you to lead. You know if you leave it up to me I'll take over." She smiled because their conversation was so easy. He may not have realized it, but she was paying him a great compliment. She never allowed anyone to lead her.

"Well, thanks for letting me lead." He smiled.

Now that she was even closer to him than she had been in the airport, she noticed that he still had the slight gap between his two front teeth. It was as cute as ever. He had aged well and that was a good thing. Still, she could see life in his eyes and some stress moments under his eyes. Those were the moments when sleep hadn't come easy for him and there was more to walk the floor over. It was all there, even the pain. She touched the place under his eye that held it tightly. Fantasy leaned her head to the side as she smoothed her finger over the place a few times until it softened a little. "That's better."

"It is better." Victor relished her touch and knew his body responded to what she wanted it to do. She took his breath away. He was coming pretty close to hyperventilating and yet he tried to regain his composure. "I was thinking that since this was just lunch we could go to the Cheesecake Factory, and someplace fancy tonight."

"That's perfect." By his selection of restaurants she knew he remembered their cheesecake nights. She had said it was perfect and, honestly, right at this moment everything was.

At the end of lunch, after sharing a slice of Godiva cheesecake, they walked out of the restaurant arm in arm. "Did you enjoy lunch?" He reached to wipe a little chocolate from the side of her mouth.

"Whoops. I thought I got that off." She reached where his finger had been. That's embarrassing. You'd think I would know how to wipe my mouth.

"It's cute and, trust me, I didn't mind at all. Fantasy, do you think it's possible to freeze time?" More than just talking about enjoying themselves, he was talking about shielding this moment, this time away from the illness. If he could somehow avoid what would be coming up in the next few weeks, how wonderful that would be.

She thought about what he was saying for a moment and nodded slightly. "I think you can keep so much of the special time with you that it never stops. You know, when something feels good and when a particular time is right, it never has to end." She slowed down and really looked at him from the side as he walked slowly beside her, holding her hand.

"You are absolutely right." He pulled her hand to his lips and kissed it.

"So tell me, what's next?" She was wired and slightly tired at the same time. It had only been three hours. "You know, we ate lunch a little later than the typical time so we likely won't be hungry for a while."

"I was thinking the same thing," Victor responded. "We could go relax a while and then go from there. I reserved a two-bedroom suite; that way we can be together and not be together."

"You think of everything." Fantasy prayed that the temptation of having him in the next room within a suite could be endured. At least if he was across the hall or two doors down she'd be less likely to sleepwalk with a purpose.

"Is that arrangement okay? If not, I can get two suites." Victor again opened the door of the car.

"No, that will be fine. I trust you." She did trust him, but trusting herself was the real issue. She had not been with anyone in a very long time. And when she had it was prior to her renewed commitment to the Heavenly Father. She had vowed that the next person she slept with would be her husband. He would be hers to keep and she could enjoy all the thrills and joys of being husband and wife.

The distance to the hotel was rather short. They talked some, but mostly they were still in awe of each other's company. For some reason, Victor was extremely nervous. Maybe he should have reserved two suites, but his only thought at the time had been to be near her as much as possible. He had no desire or intention to scare her by coming on too strong. He considered the time since he'd picked her up at the airport, and hoped that nothing he had done so far had pushed her away. His desire was to show her how much he loved her. There had to be a way to make her see that even when he was too dumb to realize it, it had been there. In essence, Victor had chased a pipe dream. He had tried to make things right and his wife had ended up caring so little about what he offered her. He didn't even think Sonya ever thought about nor considered what he had lost.

"Are you okay?" Again, Fantasy rubbed along his face, this time near his temple. She slowly caressed Victor's temple with her index finger, as if it was the most natural thing and not new to her at all. She wasn't even looking at him as she did it. Her eyes focused straight ahead, yet it seemed she knew his body so well her finger touched the exact spot it was supposed to.

"I'm fine. Why do you ask?" He glanced over at her as he pulled into the parking lot of the hotel next to the valet service.

"Just wanted to make sure. Victor, I really am okay with the arrangements you made. And we will be just fine, I'm sure of it." She smiled to reassure him. Fantasy wasn't trying to read his thoughts or feel him on that level, but that's what happened when she was really in touch with someone. Her nana said it was discernment and a gift from God.

Victor didn't know how she had just read his mind, but that was exactly what was on his mind. For a moment it freaked him out a little because she came up with that just as she was rubbing his temple. "Tell me later how you did that."

"There's nothing to tell." It was her turn to ponder. She wondered what Victor would think if he knew she had only had one lover since him. And she wondered what he would say or think if he knew that she was practicing abstinence. It wasn't like someone practicing the violin or the guitar. And on top of that, she was a grown woman. She knew she would have to tell him eventually. Fantasy had not considered disclosing it before because it was all a plan. The plan didn't include him getting close enough to smell it. It was vulgar, but true.

"Well, let's boogie, lady." He opened the door just as the bellman loaded her luggage onto a cart. Victor told him to go directly to the bay of elevators since he was already checked in.

"Have you been enjoying your stay?" The older gentleman asked Victor.

"Yes, I have. I've lived in this area but this is actually my first stay at this hotel. It's very nice." He looked around the elevator like it was his first time in it.

Fantasy smiled. He had always been a conversationalist. He could strike up a conversation with anyone who would stop long enough to listen or pause as if they were interested.

"Well, we think so too. All the comforts of home. Actually better than home. Is this a special occasion for you two?"

"Guess you can say that. We are rekindling a twenty-one-year-old flame. I wanted to do so in a very special place and I believe this is it." Victor reached for Fantasy's hand.

Again she smiled. They were walking down a long hallway and it seemed they would never get to their suite. She was taking in the sights along the way. They had passed two men coming out of a room grinning a little too hard. Then there was a young girl who looked like she was in high school and had no business being in a hotel without a parent.

Fantasy tried to look impressed. She was sure that Victor wanted to impress her and indulge her with surroundings he thought she wasn't used to. He likely thought she didn't do five stars. His thinking was her fault, because she hadn't told him the truth about what she did, even after she'd altered the plan. It seemed that time got away whenever they talked. There was so much to share. Now she honestly didn't know how to fix it. That was just one thing that she would have to make right. Hopefully, he wouldn't insult her or assume that she was outside her element. Truthfully, she was a little too sensitive for that.

"That sounds so romantic," the gentleman said.

Victor slid the card key into the slot and opened the door wide. He moved to the side and allowed Fantasy to enter first. Once she was in he moved slightly for her bags to be brought in. Once everything was in, he continued to make a little small talk as he gave the bellman a tip and closed the door behind him. He walked in to find Fantasy looking out the window at the lavish landscape and the DC skyline in the distance.

Surrounding her throughout the suite were beautiful arrangements of live flowers, and the room smelled heavenly. It seemed that she was not the only one who used oil warmers. She didn't recall telling him that little bit of information.

"I hope the flowers are not overdoing it. They didn't come with the room." Victor stopped talking. He hadn't meant to say that and hoped it didn't offend her. By the time she turned around slowly and narrowed her eyes at him he knew it was too late. He wasn't sure how she lived. They had never talked about it, but he knew that she worked in the sales department of the local paper, and, hence, probably didn't make a lot of money.

"Thanks, Victor, but I didn't think they did." She walked around with her arms folded and glanced at the floral arrangements he had selected. They were nice, but not exactly what she would have picked out. She could have easily burst his bubble, identified each flower in each vase, and told him which flowers should have really been paired together to create a balanced arrangement, a floral combination that wouldn't be too heavy in smell, as so many often were. "You did a great job and I appreciate your effort."

"I didn't mean to insult you at all. That was not my intention. I was just pointing out . . ." He stopped again. "How about something to drink?"

"No thank you." She shrugged it off and decided to busy herself with something else. "If you don't mind, I'm going to unpack and shower. I know that I wasn't in the air that long, but I'd really like to freshen up." Before he could respond she was out of the room.

Chapter 15

By the time she got out of the soothing shower, the hint of anger had dissolved. She wasn't going to let it get to her. After all, he had said he didn't mean for it to come out that way. And, as she reminded herself, she didn't exactly tell him that she knew the difference between a salad fork and a dinner fork. For all he knew she didn't. Because of all she didn't share he likely believed she hadn't been exposed to anything but the simple life. He never knew anything about her lifestyle growing up. All she had shared with him then was that her mother had died and she moved to Durham to live with her nana and granddad. They'd never met Victor, so he probably thought that they were two people struggling to raise their daughter's daughter. She'd brought to the table the limited insight he had of her, and she couldn't complain about how he served it up.

Fantasy stood in the spacious walk-in closet and went through her things. She was still thinking that they wouldn't go out to dinner. She was going to suggest that they order in and watch a movie. It concerned her that his temple was tight and he looked a little tired. She knew he'd had meetings during the two days before she'd arrived, but he had mentioned that he had cleared everything else just to spend time with her. She opted for a relaxed lounging set with wide-leg spandex heather gray pants and a pale pink ultra soft sheer tee.

All of her makeup had been removed, and she replaced it with just a little color on her lips, moisturizer, and a brush of lightweight foundation. There was nothing added to her eyes or cheeks. Fantasy looked in the mirror one last time and ran her fingers through her hair a few times.

Victor was sitting on the sofa looking at the paper. "You look nice." He knew he had put his foot in his mouth and he would have to work overtime to get it out.

"I look relaxed. I don't know if I was going for nice, but I'll accept that." She sat on the sofa beside him and crossed one ankle over the other. Fantasy smiled and handed him a beautifully wrapped small box. "Happy birthday again."

Victor folded the paper and put it to the side. "Thank you. But, before I open it, Fantasy, I'm sorry. I wasn't implying anything hurtful." He looked like he wanted to cry. He was trying to project calm, cool, and having it together when he was an emotional breed. He was hoping that she could get used to it.

"Let that go. I did; it went down the drain while I was in the shower." She leaned back farther into the comfort of the sofa and sighed. "I feel so much better and I'm ready to relax, so please just open the gift. I want to see if you like it."

Victor looked at how neatly it was wrapped. "You won't mind if I just tear into it." He was struggling, trying to get in the box.

"It's your gift." She was looking at him, not wanting to miss his reaction.

He got the bow off, tore the wrapping off, and removed the top from the white box. Inside was a long midnight blue jewelry case. He looked at Fantasy as he opened the case, and when he saw what was inside his mouth opened. "This is nice." He removed a very nice, very expensive gold bracelet that had cuts of white gold. It was indeed a handsome bracelet that looked like it cost much more than he would want her to spend. But he dared not say anything about the cost and risk offending her yet again.

"I'm glad you like it." Fantasy smiled.

"I'm putting it on right now, if you'll help me." Victor handed her the bracelet and moved his wrist toward her.

Fantasy slowly hooked the bracelet around his arm and touched it lightly. "There. It looks nice on you. I knew it would." This time she leaned in and kissed his lips.

This kiss was different. For one, it was behind closed doors; also, it was just the two of them. At first they were just enjoying the feel of each other's lips then, after a second, Victor leaned farther into her and his tongue touched hers. Instead of moving away, she pulled it farther into her mouth and the kiss deepened. She caressed his arm and he gingerly rubbed her back. When the two parted, he put his forehead against hers and they stayed that way for a minute.

"What a gift," Victor said breathlessly. He knew there was a problem below but he didn't want to look down to confirm it. How was he going to spend all this time with her and not be aroused?

"I'm glad you like the bracelet," Fantasy replied.

"I was talking about you being here and the kiss. I enjoyed that just as much. Our first real kiss in twenty-one years." Victor knew he would remember it forever, and he hoped that she would too.

"I enjoyed it too. But the bracelet is gift number one. You have a few more. My plan is to give them to you at different times throughout our time together."

"I like the sound of that." Victor kissed her again. He thought it would be a quick one, but it deepened like the first, and he forced himself to pull away while he could.

"I feel so relaxed," she said.

"So, we are going for an evening of rest and relaxation." Victor stood up. Even though he was a little slower since being ill, he still seemed to bounce off the ceiling when he started doing something or was focusing on a particular situation. He went to a bag and removed a stack of movies. "We can order room service."

Fantasy smiled. She'd conjured up the same evening before walking out of the bedroom into the suite. "Oh, you have a great collection. I don't get a chance to watch movies often. By the time I decide to go to the theatre and see something, it's out on DVD. I guess I just don't make time." She paused, realizing she was about to tell him why. It would be because of her job. That was a conversation she wasn't ready to have, so she switched gears. "So what haven't you seen? I don't want to bore you by watching something twice."

"I don't mind watching something twice. If it's something good I can watch it several times. You just pick what you want to watch."

Fantasy put her feet under her butt and went through the DVDs.

"I'll be right back." Victor left the living area and went into the bedroom he occupied. After a few minutes he returned. Fantasy was separating out what she wanted to see. He sat back down with her and smiled at her. She was looking down and he kissed her forehead.

"I can't receive without giving." He handed Fantasy an equally nicely wrapped box.

She dropped all the DVDs and grabbed the box. "I have no shame. I love receiving." Fantasy giggled, ripped the paper off, and discarded it somewhere behind her. The velvet box that held her gift was black. When she opened the box she smiled. "Great minds."

Victor reached for the box. "May I?"

"You may." Fantasy handed him the box.

He looked at both of her wrists. On one was a white gold watch with a diamond-accented band, and on the other was a tennis bracelet. He reached for the wrist with the watch, and placed the three-diamond bracelet beside the watch and fastened it. "It looks good."

He couldn't help but wonder where the expensive-looking jewelry had come from. Then he considered the fact that she was a single woman and had no kids and, thus, no one to buy for. She could likely afford nice things every now and then.

"I think it does too." She hugged his neck and kissed his cheek.

His eyes fell to the front of her tee and widened. She was much bigger there than he remembered. Her ample supply was almost busting out of the tee. They almost looked fake, but he didn't believe she would alter her body in any way. He was definitely not complaining. Victor liked everything that he saw.

"How about we go ahead and watch a movie?" He twisted his arm and looked at his watch. It was only 7:45. He could foresee one thing: it was going to be a long night.

Chapter 16

Fantasy was on her own for the morning. Victor had received an important call and would have to take care of some business that had come up unexpectedly. Of course, he wasn't delighted about the meeting. They had already planned to go to the International House of Pancakes. She chuckled when she suggested it, using the formal name rather than the just saying she wanted to go to IHOP. He had left her the car and had taken a cab, claiming he didn't have far to go.

Fantasy thought that maybe his disappearing an hour ago was more about giving her some alone space than some sudden meeting. Not that it wasn't possible, it had just come up without warning, and right after his phone rang he had excused himself. Maybe there was another woman he wanted to spend some time with.

She went to the window realizing how crazy that thought was. Since her plane had landed, Victor had been all about her. Even before he came back to the States he had been all about her. There was never any time during the day that she could not reach him, or any time that she would call the apartment or the office and he didn't talk to her. Her greatest concern then, and even now, was overindulging in the time he offered.

She was not used to twenty-four/seven unlimited, non-prohibited, unrestricted attention, and it was hard to get used to. She didn't want to admit it, but she was so attracted to this man. Whenever he got close she counted to ten and came up with something to change the chemistry between them. She didn't know how long it would work, but for right now it was working.

Of course, if they were going to go anywhere with their relationship or this foundation building, she would have to open up and share those things that bothered her. Just as he would have to share what was going on with him. There was something, and she would exercise as much patience as possible until he let her in.

She thought that that had always been the problem with relationships and getting to know someone. It required give and take and it was hard work. It seemed so sad and touching to go through all that with Mr. Almost-Right and suddenly without a sign or a warning he switches and becomes something and someone you don't recognize. Or, you assume that he will change and change doesn't come. You could move all the cheese you wanted, but if someone didn't want to change, the cheese would just be hanging out there.

What was clear to Fantasy was that she was falling for Victor even more. That first night she had fallen asleep in Victor's arms. They ordered room service and shared their late-night dinner of burgers and fries. At Victor's urging, they finished it off with chocolate molten cake. With their stomachs full, they curled up together on the sofa and watched a couple of sitcoms. They were enjoying the moment and then the conversation turned to old times. "It's time that I tell you what happened." Victor said with her snuggled up beside him. He reached for the remote and turned the flat-screen television off.

Fantasy didn't really want to talk about it but she knew that sooner or later she would have to listen to what he wanted to say; what he felt he needed to share. He had said it would help her understand what had happened between them so long ago. She told herself that it didn't matter, when, in fact, it did. She couldn't say anything; she only looked at Victor sadly and nodded.

"I know this is all hard for you to hear and it's going to be even harder for me to share. But I don't want this to be between us and I don't want you to always wonder. From the time we began to express interest in one another I really liked you. I mean, I didn't just start liking you at that point, Fantasy, I had been watching you and I kept telling myself that I was not your type. There was always something about you and I knew that you were special from the onset. I just didn't know how to approach you, especially since I was in a so-called relationship. My lucky break came when you befriended a poor soul who was in too deep and didn't know how to get out. You felt sorry for me, and while you were throwing me a line to save me from the turmoil, I could see that you cared.

"What I'm saying is that I was falling even then. It was my intention to end things with Sonya. She knew that things weren't working and she was holding on to nothing. We talked about it and she had decided not to fight me on it. By that time you and I were spending more time together and I was making promises. In my heart of hearts, I believed that I could honor each and every one. The night we made love for the first time, I knew that there was no turning back. I didn't want to turn back. I knew that we were meant to be together, Fantasy, I could feel it. I broke things off with Sonya for good after that night."

Victor looked around realizing that this was much harder than he thought. He had rehearsed what he would say and now it was difficult to get the words out. He continued, "A few weeks later she told me she was pregnant and that she had decided not to keep it. I didn't agree at all, but she wouldn't hear me. So, even though it went against everything that I believed in, I was going to pay for it. As wrong as I knew it was I began to be relieved because I could continue what we started. I wanted us more than anything.

"A week later, I received a call in the middle of the night from Sonya's parents telling me—and I do mean telling me—that she was going to keep the baby and I was going to marry her. At that point, I didn't want to disappoint my father, who told me that a man takes care of his responsibilities, so Sonya kept the baby and we got engaged."

Fantasy looked away, knowing what came next. She had known about them getting engaged and then married, but she never knew it was because Sonya was pregnant. How ironic that was.

"Before I could tell you, someone else did and you called and gave me a piece of your mind. You were so upset and furious with me. I couldn't get a word in. Before I could tell you that Sonya was pregnant and I was doing it because of the baby, you asked me never to contact you again and hung up. As much as that hurt me, I honored your wish because I felt that it was the least I could do. Despite how much I loved you, I ended up breaking your heart." This was the part where she was supposed to tell him about being pregnant. That while his daughter was growing in Sonya's belly, their son was growing in hers. She cursed him out because he was just going to up and marry Sonya without any emotional ties, nothing to connect them together. At the time, she just thought it was for love; she didn't even know he had planted his seed there too.

"I was just so upset," she said. "It was the way I found out. If I had heard it from you first, it would have still hurt, but the pain would have been a whole lot easier to bear. And, Victor, it would not have felt like you just didn't care. Honestly, I just felt like you slept with me just so you could have sex with me."

"All I could see was how much I hurt you, and I just couldn't stand to tear you apart any more than I already had. I know how you saw it, but, Fantasy, it was just the opposite." Victor tried to speak past the lump that was forming quickly in his throat.

"So, your solution was to leave me and never look back. How could you have thought that would be good for me? You were in college; I assumed you were a halfway intelligent guy." Fantasy stood up and walked across the room to put some distance between them. She patted her foot nervously and rolled her eyes up in her head. How dense could one brother be? More and more, she was feeling like he wanted his cake and to eat it, too.

"I mean, even though I laid you out at some point, you should have known it was raw emotion and reached out to me. Maybe not to console me as an almost-married man, but just to say something, anything other than just walking out like that. In all this time you never tried to look for me or see if I was okay. For all you knew, I could have died of a broken heart. I realize modern technology didn't exist and we couldn't just reach out and touch from a distance, but you could have done something. Victor, that is what hurts the most. They had you and . . ." Fantasy closed her mouth quickly; she'd almost said, "we." She didn't want to get caught up and say too much, even if it was in this kind of rage. It would accomplish little. Regardless of what had happened to her and Kam, Victor didn't need to find out like this. "I didn't." She ended it there and turned her back.

Victor almost wished that he had left the conversation for another day, another week, or maybe even another visit. He wasn't expecting it to be the easiest talk in the world, but he didn't think that she would explode. She was still hurting, and he was surprised that she was even talking to him. Her pain ran deep and now he wondered if he would ever be able to reach it and provide what was needed to start a healing. He wasn't sure what he'd expected, he just didn't expect all this. Victor had no clue that Fantasy had suffered this massively at losing him.

Victor walked over to her and wiped her tears. He kissed her eyes lightly and then each cheek. Before she could say anything or react, he picked her up in his arms. He returned to the sofa, rested his back against the cushion, and laid her body on his with her head resting on his shoulder.

"I love you, Fantasy. I've always loved you. And even when you thought I stopped, I continued. I wanted to give Niya a two-parent home. I wanted her to be happy and now I know that it was wrong. In making my child happy, I made you miserable. I thought about you, please believe that. Not just when things were bad between Sonya and me, but when things were good. You see, in those good times I thought of you because I knew with you it would have been even better. You were my everything.

"The night I received your message, my life was forever changed. I knew then that I was given a second chance, and I thanked God instantly; the same God I had once cursed because I felt that He had subjected me to a life of hell with a woman who never loved me. You gave me hope; not just in us, but a hope in God. Without God I don't think you would have ever found me. I was so far away from you and yet one message brought us together."

Fantasy's tears moistened the side of his face. He couldn't see her face, but he felt the warm tears. He felt her heart heaving in and out and knew that she needed this release as much as he needed to say all these words. It was cleansing and it was necessary if they were going to move on. He rubbed her temple and kissed her forehead. Victor held her so tightly he could feel her heart beating through his body.

"I love you more than life itself," he said

She had listened to him, and she wanted to tell him about Kameron, to stay up all night telling him all about his son. There was so much to tell and she was so proud. Fantasy knew that if she had given him a chance he would have been just as proud. All of this could blow up in her face now that she knew he'd stayed with Sonya because of a child and she had denied him a chance to get to know his other child. There was no way she could chance it. What could this mean for their future?

The truth was, Kameron wasn't going anywhere, and there was no way she could maintain a long-term relationship without the person knowing she had a son. He was twenty-one, and she couldn't change his age, either. The dead giveaway, even if the age got by Victor, was that Kameron looked just like his father. Even his fingers were like his. She remembered smiling as she held his hand and looked at his fingers. Fantasy wanted to tell him she loved him too, but it looked like it just wasn't going to work out. There was no need sharing an emotion that would be short-lived for the second time.

She would go back to just enjoying the moment and not borrowing from tomorrow's problems. "You mean a lot to me." No, she hadn't said she loved him, but it was something. It was probably not even close to what he had wanted to hear, but it was all she could give it right now. Now she didn't know what would happen next. It was a sharp contrast from what she was feeling before they had the talk. She wished he had left well enough alone. She had known she was not ready, not up for the deep conversation. All she wanted was to love this man forever and a day and then some. Why was that so difficult? And, more importantly, why was she letting what happened then affect and change things now?

She allowed more tears to fall. After a while, the continuous sound of his voice against her ear began to soothe her insides. With the feel of his hand up and down her back, Fantasy closed her eyes and went to sleep. There was hurt, confusion, and the uncertainty of accepting what he shared. But they were raw emotions and, at that moment, she sought the comfort of his embrace and presence of his love.

That was how their evening had ended. She woke up that next morning still in his love, but not knowing what to feel and in a total emotional haze.

After showering and dressing, she returned to the living room and a suite full of more flowers. Victor had slipped in, surprising her.

"You're back so soon?" She looked around the room and inhaled the sweet aroma of the mixture of flowers.

"I was halfway there when I realized that I just couldn't sit through a meeting with things between us in midair." It was true that he couldn't get the night before out of his mind. The discussion with the doctor would have to wait for another day. His health was important, but he and Fantasy working through what they were feeling was just as important. He would never again put anything or anyone before her.

"You didn't have to do that. I know how important and hard the conversation was for you. I'm sorry I exploded and handled the whole thing worse than I should have. I guess hearing it all was like pouring salt in an open wound." Fantasy sat in the chair across from him.

Victor didn't miss her selection of seating. "I wish I could take the hurt away. The only thing I can do is show you how much I love you and somehow make it up to you. If you will let me." Tears filled his eyes. Fantasy hadn't seen his tears the night before because she'd been crying on his shoulder. But they had fallen just as they were this very minute. She was not alone in the pain.

"Just let me love you." He stood up and kneeled in front of her. "That's all I ask. If after our time together you decide you can't move forward with me and with us, I'll understand."

"Okay." She didn't know what else to say. She felt his sincerity and she didn't feel alone in the hurt.

Victor squeezed her hands. "Good. How about we go get breakfast? Then maybe we can take a walk."

"That sounds like fun," said Fantasy.

They went to breakfast, took a leisurely walk, and later went to lunch at a beautiful Indian restaurant. When they came back to the room they were exhausted, and curled up on Victor's bed and took a nap.

The feel of her against his body was beyond tempting, but he held her. Victor watched her chest rise and fall as she slept, and he prayed that there would be a time when he could show her physically how much he desired her. She was his soul mate and he had always known she was a part of him. He kissed her temple softly, and in her sleep she smiled. Her dimple showed that she was happy.

"I can't believe you shopped for four hours without a break." Victor dropped all of Fantasy's bags down the minute he walked through the door.

"Stop complaining. I would still be there if you hadn't complained that your feet were hurting." She giggled as she sat down on the sofa. "Come here, sweetie, let me caress your back."

"It's not funny. You, my dear, have an addiction. Why didn't you warn me?"

"I knew you would find out in time." She kissed his lips the minute he sat down beside her. It only took a second for it to turn to something more passionate than a peck.

"How about you shower and meet me back here." Victor waited until she stood up and left the room. His manhood was pressing against his pants and he would need a few minutes before he could stand up.

She came out of the room freshly showered and dressed in a blue long, flowing gown with a slit up one side. Fantasy had oiled her body and applied lotion and body mist.

Victor was turning on the stereo just as she walked out. For a moment he could only look at her. "You look so good. Would you mind dancing with me?" Victor was dressed only in lounging pants and a tight white tank-style T-shirt.

This had been her first look at his upper body without a shirt. He had telltale signs of being an avid exerciser, and his body and torso were extremely tight. All he needed was a couple splashes of baby oil and he would have looked like some of those greased-up and greased-down models. He was really looking like a Tyson right at that moment. Fantasy had almost swallowed her tongue when he walked out of his sleeping area. She was not prepared; she had no clue. Sure, she had lain on him and felt his tight embrace, but, still, clothes covered all that up.

"What?" She looked at him with her head tilted in mystery. There had to be a catch or a joke. The things they had done in the past didn't include dancing, at least not slow. They had done the club dance thing and sweated through a bunch of dances in the heated gymnasium during his frat parties. And, if she recalled things correctly and her mind had not gone totally feeble in remembering specifics, he had very little rhythm on the dance floor.

"Victor, you can't dance." She looked at him as if she knew something that he didn't.

"Girl, I can dance." He did a quick move and threw his arm out in a John Travolta move.

"Right." She laughed at his attempt to catch a rhythm.

"Seriously. Come on." They had listened and gone back and forth during one song. "Come on, now, it's one of your favorites. Not old school, either. I just want to show you that I've been listening."

She immediately recognized the start of the song. It was Kem, and still she had not said a word. It had played softly in the background during a few of their telephone conversations. Without another word, she stood up. Victor had done his homework and captured things about her now that she thought had passed right by him. She wanted to believe it was all because he cared. She reached her hand out, and he kissed the tip of every finger before slowly folding her small, fragile hand into his large, firm one. Slowly, he pulled her in close. In the movement of the pull she felt him and tried not to jump back, but it was too late. He noticed but didn't say a word. Fantasy followed his pace in the dance, moving methodically to the rhythm he was setting. "You were saying something about no rhythm." He talked into her hair, not wanting to adjust their perfect fit.

"I must say, Victor Charles, I'm surprised," she said. They danced in silence and enjoyed the feel of one another. The night ended on the sofa again. This time, though, sometime during the wee hours of the morning, he carried her to her bed and placed her between the sheets. He wanted to join her so badly, but instead he kissed her lips softly and went to his room.

Her cell phone rang, yanking her out of her thoughts. She grimaced, not welcoming the interruption. Just as she grimaced, she considered that the caller was likely Victor, and jumped up and ran to catch the phone. After five rings it would hit voice mail. By the time she got to the living area and reached inside her bag to grab the phone, she was huffing more than a little, reminding her that she could use a workout. That's an idea, she thought as she answered without looking to see who was calling. "Hey, boo."

"Hey, Mom. How are you?" Kam's voice came through the phone line really loudly. He was talking over a bunch of voices and noise in the background. "I bet you can't guess who I had dinner with last night."

She was not expecting Kam to call; not that she had to have a set time to receive a call from the love of her life. "Hello, Kam. I'm fine, and you had dinner with Anthony." She snickered, knowing he didn't like for her to unleash a bunch of questions or answers in one snap like he often did her.

"Oh, you got jokes today." He laughed. "Yes, I did have dinner with him. Thanks for giving me time to tell my own story."

"How was it?"

"It was okay. But he was more into asking me twenty questions about you," Kam said.

"Quiz you about me?" Fantasy sat up. That was out of order. "What did he think you would say or tell him? Come on, Kam, Anthony should know that blood is thicker than water."

"No doubt." Kam chuckled.

She detested it when he talked like that. To think she was paying good money for a better-than-great education to place him among the ranks of highly skilled and trained attorneys. She smiled; her son had his own way. And she knew that it would work. "No doubt."

He laughed. "Well, old boy didn't get anything from me. We went to Legal Sea Foods and I ate some good food and ordered dessert. From there we went over to Dave & Buster's and we played pool and shot some hoops. I had some Buffalo wings. This was like a couple of hours after I had eaten and I was hungry again. And, at the conclusion, he dropped me off at my apartment and I thanked him for a lovely evening. Didn't even invite him in." Kam was cracking up with laughter.

"You are so crazy."

"Oh, before I forget, Tee sent me a photo of your new look. I like it. I even made it my phone screensaver. Brittany had to move over."

"I'm honored and touched at the same time." Fantasy was. Every time she was around Kam, he was showing her dozens of shots of Brittany that constantly rotated on his phone screensaver. To know she was getting a little screensaver action made her feel good. "I'm glad you like my new look. Did she say anything else?" Fantasy quizzed. She had sworn her to secrecy and told her in no uncertain terms not to tell Kam that she would be in his neck of the woods and that she would be meeting someone.

"Just that you were taking my nephew on a shopping spree when you get back into town. And, let's see." Kam paused for a second for effect. "And that you weren't on assignment, but somewhere meeting some man."

Fantasy almost dropped her phone. "What? I told that child not to open her mouth. What did you offer her?" She wasn't really mad; she knew Tee couldn't hold water and that her mouth opened more than a refrigerator door by a houseful of kids during the summer months. She was at least glad that he didn't know that she was in DC.

"I didn't have to offer her anything. She's my sister and I'm your son, so if you were going to check someone out, since I'm the man of the house you should have told me. There are some crazy folk out here in this world and I don't want to have to get my Glock out for no old dude who doesn't know how to step to my mother correctly. I got some boys down south who can lose anybody just like that." He was half joking, but she also knew he was just as serious as he was making light of the situation.

"First things first: I'm very selective; you know that. You can count the men I have brought into our life on one finger and you are twenty-one. I think that says a lot about what I put first. And, considering the fact that I was making a living for us and on the road a lot, it really didn't give me any time to creep. Second, I know that you are the man of the house and I should be open with you concerning my affairs, but I honestly didn't want to say anything until I knew where all of this was going." That wasn't honest at all. There was no way she could tell him that she was dating his father: the man who had left her and didn't know about him. How could she explain that he loved her but hadn't looked over his shoulder to see if she had landed on her feet?

"And, lastly, why does he have to be an old dude? I could be itching for a tender rooney or I may have decided I need a little thug loving."

"Mom, don't even joke like that. I'm not saying you can't pull one. You definitely don't look anywhere close to your age. I still keep you on lock when you come around my friends; that's for a reason. If you knew how many times I've been asked if I would be pissed if they asked you out, you would be flattered."

"Would I now?" Fantasy smiled. She was glad that she still looked young. She had Nana to thank for that. There was no way of knowing if Valerie would have held on to a youthful appearance, as she was cut out before she had a chance to age.

"You know that. Well, let me get back; the next session is getting ready to start." Kam was glad to talk to his mother. Since his engagement announcement he had planned to give her more attention than the norm.

"Okay, sweetie. Take care and I'll call you tomorrow. I don't want you to think that something has gone sour with me romancing and being romanced by old dude." She added, "I love you." She ended the call.

Fantasy had already decided early on that she was going to hit the gym downstairs. She wasn't sure how long Victor would be, but this would be the perfect way to kill some time. Afterward, she would consider going to the spa. Hopefully, by the time she had finished all that Victor would be back and they could plan their evening. A little disappointment had surfaced, but she'd traveled to DC knowing that he was in town for business. While he was gracious to make adjustments and curtail some things to give her almost all of his time, realistically she knew that wouldn't necessarily be possible. The bottom line was, she guessed, that she was just missing him already.

After a quick shower, Fantasy put on navy and key lime striped jogging pants, a navy fitted spandex tank, and white and navy Nikes. She didn't have to worry about her hair so that was a definite plus. Had that been the case her plan for today would have likely been walking through the mall, spending money; a recreational sport that required no sweating. Right before she exited her room she looked in the mirror, and she absolutely loved the woman who looked back at her. It had not always been that way, and she considered the fact that she'd achieved a real milestone and major accomplishment. She knew that so many women go through emotional drama and are not able to bounce back, or find their way back, for that matter. She definitely didn't look like all she had been through and that was a blessing. If she was one to be moved by the spirit in that way, it would be something to shout about. She was definitely down with Jesus and if it ever hit her that way, she would be like some of the church members at her home church: she'd have no problem picking 'em up and putting 'em down.

After she reached for the card key that Victor left on the kitchen counter for her, she turned and went into her purse, opened her wallet, and removed some cash. She exited the suite and closed the door behind her. There was a young attractive guy walking toward her. He was dressed in jeans and some sort of T-shirt. She could see a thick gold chain around his neck from where she was.

When he got close enough, he said, "Good morning. You sure look good."

Fantasy smiled. He really was a cute guy, probably not much older than Kam. "Thank you." She continued to walk, but was aware that he had stopped to check out her backside. She recalled what Kam had said and she grinned even harder. Maybe Victor was far from a tender rooney, and he was no thug, but he was the man she wanted. She prayed that somehow it would all pay off.

Chapter 17

Victor had been summoned to the doctor's office at 9:00. He hadn't wanted to leave Fantasy, but they said he really needed to be there. He was glad he had gone; the worst-case scenario that had been described to him wasn't his case. But they would be going forth with dialysis the next week. It turned out that his percentage of damage was not as severe as they had thought. Still, he was far from well. How his body responded would depend largely on his state of mind and his overall health otherwise. There would be diets to follow, and rest was needed, as was just cutting back on the stress and giving his all to recuperating. That really was the mandate these days for any illness. He knew that state of mind goes very far in recovery. Armed with what he had to do and some dates, he headed back toward Tyson's Corner. It was barely 12:00, so hadn't been away from Fantasy all that long.

In a few days she would be returning to Durham, and he wanted to make the most of every moment. Victor had even thought about asking Fantasy to marry him, but he knew she would turn him down. He wanted her to be over what had happened, but deep down he knew she wasn't. He also didn't peg her to be someone who really did anything on a whim, especially not something as serious as marriage. Oh, she was trying to be all risky and acting as if she was okay with no agenda, plan of action, or direction in place, and yet, like him, everything they did was planned down to the second. Even what they would watch, how long the movie would last, what they would do right after that, and how long it would take to get from here to there. Victor smiled to himself. But she tried, and he gave her an A for effort. He would allow her to grade him in that area later.

"When you said that you wanted us to get in touch with our youthful side, I didn't think we would be doing that at the zoo." Fantasy bent her head a little and looked out the front window as they pulled into the parking lot of the National Zoo.

Victor circled around a few times, trying to find a parking space that wouldn't require them to walk a great distance just to get to the front gate. There would be enough walking once they got inside.

"I think it will be fun. I haven't been to a zoo since I was in elementary school." It was true that he hadn't been anywhere near a place with lots of animals. But he was thinking it would be a carefree way of spending the afternoon. He was even excited.

"It's not the mall or one of my favorite eateries but I will give it a whirl." Fantasy glanced over at Victor, who acted like he was a kid and getting ready to go into the candy store. "You know what, Victor? I haven't been to the zoo since about that long either." The first year she had moved in with her grandparents she had traveled to this exact zoo on a school trip. She remembered being so excited.

By the time they found a parking space and walked the distance to the front gate hand in hand, they were both excited. They exchanged stories of their zoo experiences and he talked about a time in the future when he hoped he could bring his grandkids here. That, of course, caused the conversation to slow, because again his child was not Fantasy's child, and her conception she now knew for sure was the cause of their end.

The zoo was packed. They had spied several buses that obviously had kids there on school field trips. They strolled along, stopping, looking, and enjoying. Victor had also snuck his camera along and had been happily taking photos.

"How was your meeting this morning?" Fantasy looked up at him. The weather was actually great for this type of outing. It wasn't too hot and it wasn't too cool. The temperature was somewhere in the middle and she was enjoying the feel of it.

"Oh, my appointment." Victor was careful with his words. He didn't like not telling her, but he didn't feel they were solid enough for him to share yet. Of course, he couldn't explain being solid enough to consider marriage but not solid enough to share information about his illness. It was because he didn't want to be a burden or to have her worry about him. It was totally not selfish; it was all about her. "It went well. Didn't last as long as I thought. That's why I was back to the suite before you finished your morning workout."

"Oh yes, and what a morning it was. The workout was awesome. I had so much energy I was bouncing off the walls." She cleared her throat as they stopped to look at the monkeys. "I can imagine why I'd been all worked up."

"Likely it's the same reason I have been. If I thought working out would help, I would have jogged my butt down there last night, the night before that, and the night before that." He grinned wide. He had been worked up, and even in this atmosphere of sun, fun, yelling kids, and animals he was still worked up. How could he not be? Fantasy was glowing, and her beauty overwhelmed him and consumed all of him. She was all he could think about and all he really wanted to think about.

She was dressed in a beautifully printed sundress that flowed down her body. It covered almost everything, but left bare her shoulders, a small section of her back, and her arms. As with everything he had seen on her so far, it dipped slightly in the front and her ample bosom was pushed against the fabric. "I did enjoy it, and the spa was heavenly. It was worth every penny." She leaned against the fence for a second and looked at him.

"Everything you do this week is on me." Victor said it and hoped that the way he said it was okay. He didn't want her to spend money on anything.

"That's not necessary. I know how to let a man treat me, and I'll accept some things but not all. I got a little nest egg." She winked at him and started walking again. Fantasy didn't get upset about his offering. He was tactful in his approach to the money subject and that's really all she wanted.

"All righty, then. Handle your business, Ms. In Charge 2010." Victor let her hand go and stopped walking.

"What are you doing?" Fantasy turned around quickly and he snapped the photo.

Victor laughed so hard at the look on her face and how she was all ready to snap that he bent over. "That was priceless."

"And that wasn't fair." She walked back to him and hit him on the arm. "No more pictures for the next two hours."

"What? Man." Victor looked at her and pouted his lip out. The pouting was a tactic that always worked when Niya wanted her way with him. "Okay, no more pictures."

Her face softened and she looked in amazement as a clown nearby was making balloon animals. "Oh look."

She ran over to get a closer look and she enjoyed what she was seeing. Victor watched from a short distance away. She giggled, smiled, and talked to the little kids who waited for balloons. Fantasy was totally in a different element. She seemed to be so at ease with it and so happy with the moment she was in right then. He raised his camera to his eye and took several shots of her with the clown and the kids, and she didn't even notice. She had become so engulfed in the clown and his entertaining and the conversations that were being exchanged so effortlessly. A few kids had started pulling on her hand to get her attention when she was talking to another, and she would turn and give her undivided attention until another one of them desired the same.

Fantasy finally looked up and saw Victor grinning from ear to ear. She knew what he was thinking and he was entirely correct. She was enjoying the attention. It was so much better than crowded press conferences, interviews with people who cared for readers who couldn't care less, media conferences, news, news, and more news. The sad part was that much of the news wasn't as newsworthy as they thought. No one was catching the real essence of life. Rather, they were catching bits and pieces of gossip and making them stories. Life was right here in the faces of these kids, and in the face of the clown who was touched by creating artistic rubber just to put smiles on the tiny faces of the kids who surrounded him in awe. And life was watching the man she cared for and loved for a lifetime and knowing that he loved her just as much. She could see it in his eyes and it meant the world to her. The moment weighed so much more than a thousand uncertain yesterdays.

It was time to fully let the past go. It was time to tell Kam and Victor about each other, and time to tell her grandparents about the father of their grandson. They had never forced her to say and they never pressed the issue, but they shared in the responsibility of helping her raise Kameron and they deserved the truth. Their love and loyalty to her definitely had no limits. All of this needed to happen if she was going to truly live. She looked at Victor and waved her hand happily. When the kids saw her waving and who she was waving to, they all laughed and giggled and waved too.

Victor laughed while shaking his head. Kids, he thought. He waved back to the kids and blew a kiss at Fantasy.

Chapter 18

"I really wish you didn't have to leave." Victor spoke what was in his heart. "I'm afraid the past few days with you have spoiled me completely."

Fantasy looked across the table at him. They'd decided to have an early dinner at one of the popular seafood restaurants near Tyson's Corner. "I have enjoyed our time together. In the way of confession, I didn't know what to expect, but this has been much easier than I thought it would be." She was completely sincere, except regarding Victor's revelation of what had happened in the past. It was not erased by far, but they'd decided that time would be the ultimate healer.

"I agree." Victor took a bite of his stuffed flounder. It was good. Ever since the plate had been placed before him he had done little more than push the food around. He was sure that his solemn state would prevent him from detecting any flavor.

Victor was determined not to end their visit on a down note. He quickly changed the subject. "I haven't had a chance to follow current events much lately, but I read an article on the controversy about the senate seat in Florida."

Her eyes grew wide, but she didn't speak a word. She wanted to see what else he had to say about it. Maybe he was referring to an article written by someone else. A lot of reporters had covered the story; it was very hot news.

"There were a few articles, but Jordan Alexander's was totally on point."

She had just put a piece of salmon into her mouth when he said her name. The morsel of food went down the wrong way. She choked and Victor rushed to her side, thinking he would have to perform the Heimlich maneuver. Just as he moved behind her and wrapped his hands around her waist tightly, she put up a finger, signaling that she was okay. She took a gulp of water. "I'm okay." She coughed to clear her airway a little more.

"Are you sure?" Victor was still standing behind her. She had everyone's attention, but once it seemed she was okay they all resumed eating.

"Yes, I'm sure." She sipped more water as Victor took his seat. "Victor, there is something I need to share with you." She placed both hands in her lap. Fantasy looked down as she began to nervously rub her leg. "The time may not be right, but I don't want to get on the plane without telling you this."

"You can tell me anything," Victor said. He nodded in an understanding way. Of course, there would be a lot of things that they would have to share. This had been their first meeting in twenty-one years. There was something major he had not shared, so he couldn't actually say anything if she had held things back from him.

"Yeah." Just as she thought about the part she was going to tell him, she decided to tell him where she actually lived. She knew that cleverly covering the truth would have a way of making it hard to remember everything and taking the necessary steps to straighten it all out later. The thing was when the truth was covered up, there would be no intention of uncovering it later or going back to fix it. As sad as it was the compulsion to live life with small, hidden untruths and discretions because the norm and no one ever goes back to just living a life of total honesty.

"First, I don't live in Durham anymore. I actually haven't lived there in a very long time." She bit her lip slightly and looked at the window again. There was nothing there that had caught her immediate attention; she just wanted to give him a chance to listen. "I live in Ballantyne, which is on the southern edge of Charlotte." She paused again to see if he showed any familiarity with the area she mentioned. When he didn't respond, she continued. "I live there in a gated community." There may have been no need to add that, but she did, not wanting to leave anything out now that she was on the threshold of uncovering parts of her life.

"I've actually been there before." Victor glanced at her. "A friend of mine retired last year and he and wife built a home there. Country Club, right?"

"Yes." She smiled weakly.

The server walked up slowly noticing that they were in deep conversation, "Sorry to interrupt but I'll take this up as soon as you are ready."

Victor looked up and smiled. He reached for his wallet and pulled out a credit card and without looking at the bill handed it to her, "Here you go."

Fantasy smiled realizing that he was anxious to get back to their conversation.

"Why didn't you tell me that?" It was Victor's turn to reach for her hand. He wasn't sure how she could afford to live there. The smallest house in that area was still a mansion. He was almost afraid to continue to listen, thinking that she would soon be sharing that she was married or was a kept woman. "Fantasy, where you live is not even an issue." Victor chuckled a little. "No wonder you didn't act like a fish out of water when I pulled up to the Ritz. You live large."

Fantasy squeezed his hand. "Yeah, right."

"You are living large and I'm wondering if . . ." Victor stopped right there, not knowing exactly how to phrase the next part.

"You are wondering if I do anything illegal or have a sugar daddy." She smiled. This wasn't as hard as she thought it would be. But there was still a little more to tell. "No to both. I don't work for a local newspaper, either."

Her pause this time was a little long, and Victor squeezed her hand, encouraging her to go on. "Fantasy, you can always tell me anything. I love you. It may not always be pleasant and all of it may not be what I want to hear, but I promise you it can never change or damper the way I feel about you."

The server returned, Here you go and enjoy the rest of your day." She smiled.

Victor responded. "Thanks so much." He signed the slip, adding in the tip. "Let's get out of here and you can continue. He stood up, went over as Fantasy stood up and reached for her hand.

They walked out of the restaurant, hand in hand. Fantasy could feel the firm grip of his hand and she sensed that he was reassuring her that he wasn't going anywhere nor was he intending to let her go.

Fantasy hoped he meant what he had said about nothing she shared changing what he felt for her. What she was sharing was indeed small, considering that at some point she would have to tell him about Kameron. She was getting to know him again after all these years but even though they shared some history, Fantasy believed that once she dropped the news that they have a son he was going to likely flip. He already had a dark complexion but she imagined that he would turn a few shades darker than that.

Once they were seated in the car she continued, "After I left VCU, I continued my education, both undergraduate and graduate, at Duke. I was an honors student at VCU so I had no problem academically getting into Duke. My major was communications and I did work for the local newspaper in Durham for a while. I did a few jobs before taking my present job and I worked really hard at some freelance writing. Presently, I work for United Press as one of their syndicated news columnists. And my office is in my home. I don't punch a time clock. I sort of do my own thing."

Victor's eyes were wide. "Wow. That's amazing. That's not a job, sweetie, that's a serious career." Victor flipped back and forth mentally in his memory Rolodex, trying to remember if he had seen her name anywhere. If she worked for United Press, that meant she had national exposure. And he would have heard her name before. It was, of course, a one-of-a-kind name.

Fantasy slowly smiled again, knowing what he was thinking. "I decided after I left graduate school that a name like Fantasy Whitman wouldn't really fly in the media industry, so I use an alias when I write."

"Oh, okay, that makes sense." Victor continued to stare deep into her eyes. It didn't matter what came out of her mouth, he was totally in awe of Fantasy and everything about her life mattered. Since it did he would get over or around any hurdle that presented itself. "So what's your name? Let's see how good you really are. You've got to be good if you're national."

"I've been told I'm pretty good. I have never blown my own horn. But there are some who say that I'm at the top of the game." That was the truth. And she had the money and prestige to prove it. "My name is Jordan Alexander."

Thankfully, they were in a parking space, because Victor spun around toward her. "What? Jordan Alexander?"

"Yes, that's me, Victor." Fantasy looked at his silent form for a few minutes and tried to see what he was thinking. The silence was killing her. He didn't really look like he was mad at her, but he didn't seem elated either.

"Oh my God. I would have never guessed. I mean, I've never seen your photo anywhere. I have followed you religiously." He paused. "I told you that when we were having dinner. That's why you choked."

"I couldn't believe you were telling me that you like my style." She touched his face. "I was so flattered. I wanted to say something then, but when you didn't have to save my life and you returned to your seat, we immediately started talking about something else."

"You could have interrupted me. I would have had no problem shifting to another topic, like, 'Hey, Victor, I'm Jordan.'" He laughed. "But, as I said, I understand, and I'm not upset in the least bit. How can I be? I'm glad that you have done well and that you have accomplished so much. Here I thought you were impressed with me being among an elite group of command chiefs." He touched her leg gently and smiled. He was in the presence of a woman that had it all together and among everything else he knew, she was a complete package. And he prayed she would be his one day soon. "You are a wonderful woman and I'm impressed with you before this moment and now." Victor pulled out of the parking lot and headed to the airport.

"Victor, I am impressed by how many years you have served your country proud. There is no way that what you do pales in comparison to what I do. At the end of the day, it's really just a job. In fact, I'll let you in on a secret." She leaned in closer toward him. "It's not as exciting as it used to be." Fantasy became serious. "For a while, a long while, I had been so committed to what I do. It was everything; a very real extension of who I am. Then, right around the time that I discovered you, I realized that something was missing in my life. Come on, I was in the middle of an assignment and I'm chatting it up on a social network. That says something about my commitment lately. If I had remained on the grind the way I had been just two weeks before I discovered you, it wouldn't have happened. I had no time for anything or anyone if it had no direct correlation to what I do."

"Somehow I know what you mean." Victor did. There was, of course, the illness, but he had decided that after it was all said and done, retirement would be his next assignment. It was time for him to figure out the "what next" of life. And he wanted to do that with Fantasy.

"I can't believe the week has gone by so quickly. I guess time really does fly when you are having fun," Fantasy said. She was looking out the window, but felt the need to break the silence.

Both of them were sad that their time was coming to an end. Somewhere in the midst of their sadness, though, there was some excitement knowing that it was only the beginning. The two of them were working on a merger and had decided to work hard on building a solid foundation.

When she learned that Victor's time in the States was being extended so he could work on a special project at Andrews Air Force Base, she was elated. They would be able to visit one another as often as they wanted. She was especially pleased because her flexibility would work wonders for spending time with Victor. Now that he knew she designed her own schedule and didn't punch a clock, they had all the time in the world.

Fantasy reached over and touched his hand, which was situated on the gearshift. She glanced over at him and watched his jaw stiffen. He was chewing a piece of gum and focusing on the interstate traffic, but behind his sunglasses there was more going on than staying with the flow of the vehicles on the road. He felt what she felt, she knew that. But there was something else going on.

They chatted about her confession while they navigated through the airport. By the time they got situated, she had about forty-five minutes to wait. "That was like a marathon."

"It's crazy how long it takes these days to get through the airport. Nine-eleven did a whammy on everything."

Fantasy agreed with a nod, and then she saw them. She couldn't believe it, but Kam and Brittany were coming her way. "I have to go the restroom. I'll be right back."

Victor looked at her, stunned. She jumped up and walked away before he could even ask her if she was okay.

Her attempt at a getaway didn't work. She heard her son call out to her just as she turned her back. Maybe if she had been a minute or two quicker in her retreat she wouldn't be facing what was to come.

"Mom." Kam sped up to get to her. They stood just a short distance from where she had been sitting with Victor.

She couldn't just keep on walking like she didn't see or hear him. Stopping with her back still to him, she prayed. Fantasy turned around slowly and faced her son. She wanted to look to see if Victor was looking in their direction, but even without that confirmation she knew he was. "Hey." Her voice was as soft as a whisper. She didn't know why she was talking so low; it wouldn't exactly make her invisible.

Kam hugged and kissed her first, and then Brittany followed suit. "What are you doing here? I thought you were still hanging out with old dude."

"I was." She stuttered over her words. "Now I'm on my way back home." Finally, she looked in Victor's direction, and he gave her a questioning look.

Victor didn't know what to think. He'd clearly heard the young man call her Mom. He knew that she was a friendly person, and she had mentioned doing things in the church. Maybe this young man was somewhat of a godchild. That would make what he'd heard sensible.

Just as Victor was trying to understand the scene and the two main players, something happened. Kameron turned toward him, and, for the first time since he had been standing there talking to Fantasy, Victor saw his face. There was instantly something familiar. He was trying to respect her privacy by remaining in his seat, but there was a force that pulled him; he needed to go over to them. Before Victor could totally ignore it, he yielded and walked toward the threesome.

Fantasy saw him coming and took a deep breath. She tried to smile. Maybe she could somehow come up with something, anything.

Victor came over and stood next to her. "Fantasy, who is this handsome young man?" Victor's eyes were locked on Kameron's face. The pull he felt inside was even stronger now.

Kameron moved forward a little and extended his hand. "Kameron Whitman, sir." He smiled. "And this is my fiancée, Brittany Peters."

"Hello," Brittany said, and extended her hand.

Victor spoke up. "It's very nice to meet you both. I'm Victor Charles." He waited to see if the name meant anything to Kameron. When it obviously didn't register, he decided to add more. "I'm an old friend of Fantasy's."

Still nothing. He moved closer to Fantasy, who hadn't moved a muscle or said a word. Yet her face confirmed what he was thinking. Victor continued. "We went to VCU together, oh, what, Fantasy, twenty-one years ago?"

Fantasy answered. She was pissed that Victor added the extra number of years since they were college sweethearts. He really didn't have to go that far. If he would have just waited and given her a chance to send Kameron on his way, she would have sat down and told him everything. They both deserved much more than meeting for the first time in the middle of an airport. "Yes, I think that's correct."

"Mom doesn't talk much about her time there. But I've heard great things about the school. I graduated undergrad at Duke and I'm in law school there as well." Kameron was proud of what he had accomplished. Being a conversationalist—and one who was never at a loss for words, much like his father—he continued. "I'm on an internship right now as a page on Capitol Hill."

Victor would have sat down if there had been a chair close enough. This had all knocked the wind out of him. His son (although that part had not been confirmed) and his daughter attended the same school. Who knew how often they were walking the campus grounds around each other? What if he hadn't met this pretty young lady, Brittany? What if they had ended up having a fling and Niya had gotten pregnant by her brother? Victor had to brace himself to keep from falling down. He tried to sound calm and cool. "What wonderful accomplishments. I know your mother must be very proud of you." He turned to Fantasy.

Since the start of this reunion, she had said hardly anything. She just stood, looking like someone had pulled the rug out from under her. "I am very proud of him."

Before another exchange took place, Brittany looked at her watch. "Kameron, we'd better go. My flight will be boarding in a few minutes."

Fantasy wanted to know where the heck her plane was and why it had not come, say, ten minutes ago?

Brittany spoke up, noticing how Fantasy was looking at her. "I'm going to visit my sister in California. I was here visiting my sweetheart for a few days." Money afforded her the luxury of flying all over the place at will. She was actually working for her father in his medical office until she started her physical therapy program.

"Oh, I see." As much as she loved her son, she needed him to be on his way. She didn't know what exchange she and Victor would have, but she wanted it to happen and be over. "Well, have a nice time."

Kameron moved close and embraced his mom tightly. He could tell that this was awkward for her, he just didn't know why. He whispered to her, "Are you okay?"

She tilted her head to look up at him. "I'm just fine, sweetie." It was forced. She knew that she and Victor would never be fine after this.

"Well, call me the minute you land." He kissed her again and turned his attention to Victor. The interrogator in him kicked in, and he knew that something about this old dude wasn't right. He had never seen his mother this nervous. She was uneasy about him meeting her mystery man. He had a few questions, and couldn't understand the feeling he was having at coming face-to-face with him. He wouldn't concern himself with it right now. One thing was always true with him and his mother: if something didn't sit well with one of them, they always talked about it. Nothing was ever left to be categorized as confusing, nor as issues that would leave either misinformed. So, with that history to go on, he decided to wait.

"It was very nice to meet you, Mr. Charles." Kameron smiled. As he was saying good-bye though, he realized that there was something familiar about this man. He knew that he hadn't seen him before, at least, not that he could remember.

"You too, Kameron. I hope to see you again soon." That was the God's honest truth. He wanted to see him again.

Brittany had stood there like she had seen something that just wasn't right. As a woman, she had that intuition thing going on, and there was something that was in this unexpected meeting that was out of sync. She had watched Fantasy's body language and it was as if she wanted to vanish. That was unusual for Kameron's mother; anytime she had a chance to be in his company, she was always happy. It was especially strange considering that this chance meeting had happened in DC.

The young couple waved good-bye and headed in the direction where Brittany's plane would be boarding. A few times, Kameron looked over his shoulder as if he needed to get another look to confirm whatever he thought he saw or didn't see. Each time he smiled and waved.

Victor didn't waste any time at all. "Fantasy, is Kameron my son?" He didn't look at her.

"Yes." It was only one word, yet it answered his question and changed their worlds. The heat she felt inside moments ago that had reached a boiling point now turned to ice. Her entire body shivered from pain, anger, and sadness.

"I can't believe this." Victor walked on numb legs to the seat he had vacated minutes before. His eyes were fixed and he stared straight ahead. He wasn't focusing on anything and, truthfully, he felt blinded by all that had transpired.

Fantasy sat beside him and was careful not to touch or brush up against him. She knew he wasn't the violent type, but she wasn't sure if this whole scenario could cause him to snap. "I don't know what to say."

"I do. Why didn't you tell me?" Victor looked at Fantasy. There was disappointment where earlier there had been love and admiration. "I deserved to know that I have a son."

She didn't want to dance around this. It was out now and she was going to be upfront with him. "Isn't it obvious why I didn't tell you?" There was more bass in her voice than usual. He was coming out of the box on her when she wasn't the one who had orchestrated the reason she couldn't share in the first place.

"No, actually, it's not obvious. There was no reason, none at all, why you should have kept him a secret. I had every right to know," said Victor.

She felt his anger unleashed on her, and, while she was trying to take a different avenue, she would just speak her mind and let the chips fall. "I can't believe you are sitting here like you stayed around long enough for me to have told you anything. In case you've forgotten, you made your choice and you moved on without telling me a thing. I didn't even get a good-bye. No 'Dear, Fantasy' or anything.

"I found out I was pregnant a week before I was told you were marrying Sonya." She felt the familiar pain of that time and how it had all unfolded. "You'd made a choice, and while I had no idea you did so because she was pregnant, there was no way I would use my child to hold on to you. And I didn't want my child to be the reason you didn't do what you wanted to do."

"You should have told me. It was my choice to make." He still didn't move or turn toward her.

Tears began to fall from Fantasy's eyes. The salty taste of her own tears touched her lips. "After I found out about the engagement, I did call. I was going to tell you about our baby. The one thing I asked you was if you loved me. Victor, you didn't answer me. I waited for what seemed like an eternity and you couldn't even tell me you loved me. So, yes, I blew up and, yes, I cussed you out. But what did you expect?"

Victor immediately remembered her asking him over and over if he loved her, and he just hadn't been able to answer. "I had to marry Sonya, and telling you I loved you would have made matters worse."

"What could have been worse, Victor? You walked away from me and our unborn son."

"You still had no right to keep him from me. I am his father and it has taken me twenty-one years to learn that I have another child." Victor couldn't see past his pain. "It was not your decision to make alone."

"Then whose decision was it? You made it a solo project. You could have talked to me after I calmed down, after I had completely lost it because of the hurt and pain, but you never even looked back. Love would have made you push your selfish feeling aside and your worry of being cussed out again, but it was just easy for you to chalk it up to 'she doesn't want me in her life' and ride off into the sunset. The truth is, if you and Sonya were still living happily ever after, you wouldn't be here. You likely would have never responded to my message. So, play the victim in this, Victor, but the only victim—I repeat, only victim—is the caring, passionate, and loving man you met a few minutes ago."

"I married Sonya because my dad would have been disappointed in me. He expected me to be strong and to own up to my responsibilities." Once those words escaped his lips, even in his solemn state of mind he wished he could take them back.

"How would your father have felt if he knew you had gotten me pregnant as well? What would he have told you then, Victor? To marry us both?" Fantasy stood up. "I didn't want you to do to me what you just said you did to her: marry out of obligation." Fantasy felt like the wind had been taken completely out of her sails.

"I was obligated to do what was right. And all these years have passed, and Niya had a right to know that she had a brother." Victor didn't know what was going on. Every time he opened his mouth, nothing seemed to be coming out right. It all sounded right when it flowed through his mind, but once it was out, something happened.

"Please don't feel that you have an obligation to Kameron now that you know, because you don't. And why is this about Niya? For her twenty-one years of life, she has had you." Fantasy reached for her tote and her purse. "You know, I was thinking that this was not the right time or the right way for you to learn that we share a wonderful son. Now, I'm thinking that while the way was not ideal, the timing couldn't have been better. It has kept me from making the second biggest mistake of my life."

She didn't zero in on him to see if he was looking at her, or the floor, or somewhere else. Fantasy walked away toward the gate. This time she was the one who didn't look back.

Chapter 19

It had been nine weeks, six days, twelve hours, and eight seconds since she walked away from Victor at Dulles Airport and Fantasy still ached. At first, it was just her heart breaking. Then she couldn't think clearly. Then she felt the stabbing all the way to her soul. During the fourth week into the pain, her physical body followed, and she finally succumbed to the agony and had surgery on her back to relieve the pain.

Fantasy moved slowly to the kitchen. She removed from the oven the lasagna she'd made, placed it on the counter, and inhaled the great aroma. Placing the oven mitts down beside the popping-hot glass casserole dish, she dabbed at her eye. She had planned to cook for Victor on his first visit to see her. Fantasy had mentally prepared for the evening, from the flowers that she would strategically place throughout the house—and especially in the guest suite—to the menu. She had even thought about the after-dinner music she'd play as they danced in the glass-enclosed patio. It would have been so romantic. She envisioned him holding her tightly in his arms under the moonlight.

Once she moved toward the breakfast nook, she sat in a chair. Fantasy folded her hands together and looked out the window. It had been this way since the day she left Victor at the airport. He invaded her thoughts every minute and every second. The nurse had asked her in the recovery room if Victor was the name of her significant other, because she had called out for him as she was coming out from under the anesthesia.

What should have been getting better was actually getting worse. After talking to her pastor, she decided it was time to uncover all that was hidden deep inside. After that, she would take a vacation away from everything and everyone, except Nick. The two best friends would soon be spending two weeks in Jamaica.

As was his norm, Nick made a noisy entrance.

"Hey, girly girl. What's good with ya?" Nick walked over to where she was sitting and kissed her forehead. He carried two bags over to the counter and began to unpack them.

"Did you get everything?" Fantasy asked as she walked up behind him.

"I got everything on your list, plus a few things that weren't on your list but should have been."

"So you say." She knew he was probably right.

Since the surgery, and, actually, even when she called him from Dulles that day, he had become even more concerned and more protective. He blamed himself in part, saying that he had been so wrapped up in his affair that he wasn't as involved in her affair as he should have been. She, of course, chastised him, saying that she didn't need him to be her keeper.

"Yep, I say." He chuckled, putting the last item away.

"I was just thinking about our vacation. I'm starting to get excited."

"I'm excited myself. A free trip to Jamaica just to watch Ms. Fantasy. " Nick thought about the movie Driving Miss Daisy. It's a sweet deal. I figure I can take you out to play bingo, let you do a little sightseeing, go to a few bazaars and get your shop on, not to mention feed you a few times. With all that, I should be putting you to bed by eight o'clock, right after a warm glass of milk. Then I can hang out."

"You are not funny." She was laughing so hard her side was beginning to hurt. "That will not be my itinerary. I plan on having a good time and, who knows, I may just get my groove back." She snapped her fingers, and moved and wiggled the part of her body that would cooperate.

"Don't hurt 'em, Stella," Nick said. He was joking, but he really did want her to have a good time. She deserved so much more than the hand she had been dealt. He really thought that things would have worked out with Victor. He still couldn't believe that he had blamed Fantasy for not telling him, when he clearly made a choice and it did not lean toward his best friend. Fantasy must have known what was on his mind, because the morning after she had forbidden him to contact Victor or to send his boys out to bring him back to Carolina and give him a beat down. He was not totally sold on not saying anything or not getting involved. Nick had used his sources to find out where Victor was. It appeared that he was still at Andrews. Depending on how this latest intervention to restore what Fantasy had lost went, he figured he might be making a special trip to see Victor Charles. And he personally cared little about his rank.

"I just want to get away." Fantasy stood up and removed plates from the glass-front cabinet. "Scratch that. I need to get away. Nick, I'm miserable and I can't live like this. A part of me wants to run to him and a part of me wants to cuss him out. It's sort of like not being able to live with him and not being able to live without him."

"Well, I think this time away should help. I feel it in my spirit." He was trying to turn the situation to light instead of heavy. While she busied herself with getting glasses, he got the silverware.

"All right, Benny Hinn." Fantasy couldn't believe his humor. In the worst of situations, he could make her laugh.

"So, is Dee still okay with you joining me? Wait a minute, let me put it the way you put it, watching Miss Daisy."

"She is. Of course, she would love to be with big daddy. You know me on the sand and in the blue water." Nick was rubbing down his chest with his eyes closed.

"Do I need to get the hose?" Fantasy began to shake her head. Nick was too much. She knew the extra comedy scene was to keep her uplifted. He just didn't know that she didn't feel up to laughing. "Well, I don't want her to be upset with me for taking you."

"You are my best friend and she understands our special relationship. And that's saying a lot, because you know not many women I've been involved with understood how we are. Seriously, Fantasy, you need me and I'm there. End of story. And if Dee had a problem with that and if she were threatened by you in any way, I wouldn't be able to stay with her."

"I'm glad she understands." Everything was ready for the family dinner. The only thing that wasn't homemade was the dessert. The strawberry and lemon parfaits had been delivered by one of the local bakeries. She was a little nervous because this was an uncovering dinner. Since Kameron was in Durham for Brittany's family reunion, it was the best time, and it would be right before she left for her last effort sanity restoration.

“So everything’s ready?” Nick asked now, because he heard a vehicle pull up and knew it was the family.

“Yes.” She wanted to tell Nick about her decision to tell her son about his father in the presence of the people she loved the most. But she didn’t, just in case she had a change of heart. She prayed that she wouldn’t, because it was long overdue.

“I am. Nick, I’ve decided that it’s time to put everything in the open and I’ll deal with whatever consequences come. It’s just time. In fact, my friend, it’s way, way overdue.” Fantasy inhaled and exhaled slowly. Yoga had become a part of her healing process. She had started two weeks ago and she wasn’t sure yet if it was working.

The front door opened and everyone was headed their way, laughing and talking.

“It smells good up in here.” The mixed aroma of foods filled the kitchen, dining area and flowed throughout the rest of the lower level of the house. Kameron came around the island, leaned down, and kissed her cheek. Normally he would have hugged her, but he didn’t want to chance touching her in the wrong place. “Hey, Mother dearest.”

“Hello, my son.” Fantasy moved slowly away from him and kissed and hugged Brittany. “Hey, daughter.” Their relationship was off to a wonderful start. It was Brittany who had spent the three nights with her while she was in the hospital. And she volunteered to assist Nana an entire week when Fantasy first came home. While there may have been a few drawbacks, which mostly had to do with her taking Kameron away, she realized that Brittany had a good heart and she knew that she would work hard to make Kameron happy. This she had shared with him during one of the many evenings that she had taken her happy pills, otherwise known as pain meds, and was feeling all emotional and deep, like suddenly every thought she had was profound.

As soon as Nick finished kissing her grandparents, she took her turn. "Hey, Nana." She gave her grandmother a slight hug.

"Hey, sweetheart, how are you feeling?" She looked around the kitchen. "I hope you didn't overdo it."

"I didn't. I have had a pretty good week." She smiled as if to reassure her.

"Granddad, you are looking mighty handsome. Is that a new shirt?" Fantasy walked up to him and smoothed the front of his shirt. "And you smell all good."

"Oh, thank you, precious. Your grandmother went shopping the other day with some of the women in her missionary circle. Which was, in itself, better than them sitting around every other Wednesday gossiping about the folk in the church and everybody they know in the community."

"Matthew, you need to stop. You know good and darn well we don't be talking about folk." Nana put her hand on her hip. Then she thought for a second. "Well, there may be one or two who don't know how to mind their business."

"See, I told you." Matthew started laughing, and took a seat next to Kam.

The kitchen buzzed with family joy and Fantasy felt so blessed. By the time they had finished dinner and Nick was serving parfaits all around, Fantasy decided it was time.

"Guys, there is something that I need to share with all of you." She placed her cloth napkin on the table.

"I've been through some things lately, both with my health and in my personal life. All of it has caused me to stand back and evaluate some of my decisions. And, truthfully, I wasn't happy with some of the decisions I have made. There are things I wish I had done differently, things I wish I had said, and while we don't know what our tomorrows hold, I would never want to leave this earth and not say or share what I should have." Fantasy felt herself choking up.

Kameron cleared his throat and asked her slowly, "Mom, ah, did you take a happy pill before we got here or any time since we've been here with you?" He noticed that she was entering the deep and profound zone and wondered if she had dipped into the pill bottle.

"No, Kam." She giggled. "I'm fine and not feeling good from the drugs."

"Good. Please go on." Kam sat back in his chair and Brittany playfully tapped his arm.

"There are things that I have covered up for so long. I had emotionally detached myself from so many things." She swallowed. "Kam, I never talked about your grandmother, Valerie, when you were growing up, because the day she was killed I covered up everything about her and all that surrounded her life and how it all ended up. Up until I came to live with Nana and Granddad, I was exposed to a life that no child should be exposed to. I was taught things by my mother that no young girl should be taught. She didn't care that the morals she was instilling in me weren't right. She simply cared that if I followed her lead and lived my life by the mold she had set for me, I'd be okay. I'd be a survivor and I'd always land on my feet, as she would put it. Her measuring stick really wasn't being rich in friendships, family values, or anything like that. It was simply money. The more she had, the more secure she felt in life. That wouldn't necessarily be all bad, but it was the way she got her money that was a problem."

Her grandmother had already started crying silently. Kam looked at his mother.

"Kam, your grandmother was a prostitute. And because she was really smart and could have been anything else she wanted to be, she started a business employing other prostitutes. She purchased two row houses in Brooklyn, one we lived in and one she worked out of. Her empire did very well and she catered to some very prominent business men; some were in the highest positions in New York, New Jersey, and Philadelphia. By the time I was ten she owned the whole block and we were living large. It was around that time that she decided to begin my training in the business."

Nana grabbed her chest. "Oh, my God, no."

"No, Nana. I was too much like her and had too much fire just to obey. When she decided to put me out there I convinced her that I would do much better learning the business end first, and then I'd work the street. She didn't like it, but she agreed. When she tried again it was one of her older workers who stood up for me and made Valerie back down. It was a terrible life, and to keep from being teased in the neighborhood, I acted tough. I was heading down the same road until one early morning.

"She was driving to Long Island for one of her regulars. She would tell me he was worth the personal visit and he was too high up to be seen in our area. I'd been there before so many times. While she went to one area of the large house I would go in this large living room and watch television. But on that day, when my mom went upstairs and I had settled down in the living room with the remote, a lady came in, and she looked at me and didn't say a word. I didn't know who she was and thought maybe she was his housekeeper or something. After a minute, I heard voices and screaming and yelling. There were some shots and then the same lady came downstairs, laughing. She was covered with blood and she walked out the door holding a gun and laughing her head off. I ran upstairs. The whole area smelled so strange. The door was closed a little, and I walked up to it slowly and pushed it all the way open. There was blood everywhere, and Mom was lying in the bed with her naked body only partially covered. He lay on the floor, face down. I knew I should have walked out; I knew that I would never recover from what I was seeing. Even at ten, I knew it would stay with me forever." Fantasy was trembling.

Kam reached over to cover her hand with his, and he cried.

"I walked closer, Kam, and her eyes were open, but she didn't look scared. I heard somewhere that when people are killed and they are aware that it is happening they have a look of fright. That wasn't the case with Valerie. She just looked hard. There was a gunshot in her forehead and there was blood all over the sheet, so the lady must have shot her some other places. I stood in that room just looking at her. Then I reached out and pulled the bloody sheet over her.

"The woman that had come in was his wife. In a jealous rage brought on by my mother being his lover, she decided to kill him and her. The cops came, but I never knew who called them. They took me away and called Nana."

Brittany spoke softly. "Oh, my God."

"Because of that, I was never the same. I didn't have any concept of love or loving until I went to VCU. Then I met someone and I fell so hard I hardly knew what had happened to me. I, the person who had been hard core and taught on the streets of Brooklyn, fell hard. He saw a different person than the one I had portrayed. I wasn't worried about how hard I fell because he told me that he was in love with me. Kam, I felt like I had fallen in a soft place." Fantasy smiled to herself, remembering one of the gifts that Victor had given her when they were together in DC. He gave her a beautiful white stuffed teddy bear, and what was so special was that he had placed an ID charm around the bear's neck that said SOFT PLACE.

"The problem was that he was not just seeing me; there was someone else. But of course he promised he was going to break it off. I believed him. By the time I had shared my most precious gift and was playing the waiting game with him, I found out that I was pregnant. In that same space of time I learned that he was marrying the other person. Of course I went to him and cussed him out and I prayed he would say I was wrong, that what I'd heard was wrong. He didn't. He claimed that I didn't give him a chance to say anything. I felt his confession of loving me should have just come out, between my bursts of outrage. When he said nothing, I told him I never wanted to see him again and walked away. I decided that I would not use my unborn child as a pawn to get him back. If he wanted to marry her, I wouldn't beg him not to. But I waited and prayed that he would come after me. I just wanted him to change his mind. He didn't. It wasn't until recently that I found out the other girl was pregnant, and that's why he married her. The wonderful part is that I gave birth to a wonderful son, and he grew up to be a great man."

Kam was still holding her hand, and at times he tightened and other times his other hand caressed her cheek as tears fell down her cheek. "Mom, it's okay. I have had a wonderful life."

"I know that. We have done well. Not just me but everyone around this table has done well with raising you. But a man needs to know his identity. And I love you for never asking and loving us enough not to want to know. Sweetie, I can't keep it from you anymore. And know that, before I tell you, it's not because I want you to reach out to or embrace him in any way. Although, if that's your decision, I won't stop you. This is your call and I respect and love you enough to know that you will do what's right for you, your future wife, and the grandkids that he and I will have." Fantasy looked around the table, and all eyes were on her.

Nick nodded and smiled slightly, letting her know that it was okay to go on.

"The man you meant at the airport, Victor Charles; Kameron, he is your father." She watched his face and she tightened her grip on his hand, waiting to see if he would snatch away or fly off.

"Really? Wow." That's what Kameron said.

Brittany touched his shoulder and smiled. "Wow."

Fantasy continued, "I met him in DC because we connected on Facebook a month or two before and we sort of picked up on the feelings that were still very much alive. Even after we reconnected, I decided not to tell him about you. I don't know why, perhaps for the same reasons I didn't tell him back then. When he saw you he knew instantly. The thing is, he felt I should have told him and that I was in the wrong. Maybe I was, in part, but it's hard to be a part of someone's life and to add a baby to the mix when they are exiting from yours. So we discontinued what we were restarting."

"Mom, you still love him?" Kam asked.

"That's not important." She smiled. "But, as for Victor Charles, he's from a small town in Virginia. He is an only child, his mother still lives there, and his father died when he went into the Air Force. He enlisted the year he left VCU. He is divorced; I almost forgot to add the best part." She laughed through her tears.

"That's awful. You shouldn't say that," Pearl chastised, but felt the same way her grandchild did.

"Yes, she should," Matthew spoke up. "Yeah, I said it and I'm still saved."

Fantasy continued, "He has a daughter named Niya, who is a medical student at Duke."

"Man. Now that's crazy." Kam looked around the table. "I've probably seen my sister all over campus and didn't know she was my blood."

"He's been stationed all over and is Master Sergeant Command Chief for one of the wings in Ramstein, Germany. Kam, I don't want you to be hardhearted toward him. What happened, happened between us. And the man I know, the man I fell in love with, loves you. If he's upset about anything concerning my decision, it is because I cheated him. Because I didn't afford him time with his son." Fantasy fell silent when it was all out and felt completely drained. She had hoped that Kam would say something but nothing came quick.

Nick moved and spoke first. "Fantasy, I am so proud of you, and I think I speak for everyone. But I also think you need to go and lie down for a while."

"I think I will." Fantasy stood up slowly.

Nana and Granddad came close and each of them hugged her and kissed her face. Nana spoke for them. "We love you. What you did took a lot of heart and a lot of courage. Heart and courage that you got from your mother. Never be ashamed about where you came from. She gave and shared love the only way she knew. It didn't start off that way. I'm not sure how Valerie got it mixed up, but she loved you with her heart. Somewhere along the way that heart turned dark and she never gave anyone a chance to turn it back. Don't let that happened to you." She kissed Fantasy's cheek again and smiled. "You have uncovered and now you need to live."

Fantasy nodded, and walked toward her room with Nick right behind her. Once she was settled with pillows in all the right places and a throw over her legs, she relaxed. She reached for the remote and flipped through the channels. "I thought he would have said something else or asked me some questions. I guess I should be relieved and happy that he didn't lay me out."

"He would never do that. But the questions will come. Just give him time." Nick kissed her forehead and turned to walk out the door.

Just as she was ready to drift off, there was a light knock and Kam walked in. He didn't say a word until he was lying next to her on the bed. "I felt something when I saw him at the airport. I knew there was something special about him. I just didn't exactly know what. I'm not upset with you at all, I could never be. And the truth is, I'm not upset with him and I feel like that's disserving you."

"It's not, Kam. I can't expect you to hold the same view. I have reasons and you really don't. Neither of us knows what he would have done with the truth that I was carrying you."

"True." He breathed. "I want to get to know him if that's okay with you. I don't want to be his son instantly. I mean, I'm not trying to call old dude Dad or anything like that. At least, not right away."

"I expected you to tell me that. That's who you are and the kind of person you are. I have a feeling that once you reach out, both of you will find the right way to fit into each other's lives."

"You think?" he quizzed.

"I'm sure of it," Fantasy replied.

"Well, tell me. If you have all of this figured out, why have you not figured out how you two can get over the past and the differences concerning me, Niya, and even his ex-wife, and realize that you two are likely better together? I'm sorry, as miserable as you've been since you left DC, he is likely just as miserable, if not more. Old dude is probably kicking himself that he messed up the new thing you two were starting."

"You think you know so much." She punched his side.

"I think that if you love him you need to give all this up and be with him." Kam kissed her cheek and got up. "I'm out of here so you can sleep. We all know where to lay our heads, so don't worry about us. In fact, Nana and Granddad have already retired."

Fantasy started laughing. She had to hold her sides so it wouldn't hurt her back.

Kam laughed, but didn't even know what he was laughing about. "What's up, Mom?"

When she could finally talk, she said, "Oh nothing. I was just wondering if Granddad took his pill."

Chapter 20

"Oh, this is truly paradise on earth." Nick walked in from the balcony dressed in white linen pants and brightly colored button-down short-sleeve shirt.

"I know, isn't this just the best place?" She was laid out on the sofa, reading a novel by Carl Weber, her favorite author, enjoying the villa. "I've been to the island before, but this is the best place I've stayed. You know, I'm feeling real guilty. I wish you had brought Dee."

"I know she would have liked this place. But this is about us. Me and you. Friend and friend. Thing one and thing two. Besides, we can come again once you work out your relationship issues." Nick chuckled. He walked over to the chair across from the colorfully printed sofa she was stretched out on. Reaching to the center table between them, he picked up a glass and poured iced tea into it.

"I don't have relationship issues." She stopped reading, and looked at him over the edge of the book cover and over the frame of her glasses. "You are implying that I was in a relationship. I don't think the stunt I pulled with Victor could ever be considered a relationship." She sat up slightly, removed her glasses, and put the book to the side. "Isn't there like a certain time limit that denotes when you can label what you are in as a relationship?"

"I'm sure there is, or maybe there isn't." Nick looked confused.

"I thought you had answers to everything," she joked, and got up off the sofa. Fantasy needed to move around to keep her back in motion.

"How about we take a walk?" Nick noticed that she moved around a little slower than she had earlier.

"Sounds good. Let me change and I'll be ready. We can probably go grab some dinner while we are out. How about we try the restaurant we walked past a few days ago?" she yelled back to him from the bedroom she was occupying.

As she was dressing, her cell phone beeped, letting her know she had a voice mail. The reception here was up and down. But she wasn't taking any assignments, and everyone in her family had the number to the villa, so she didn't feel she needed to keep her phone on her all the time. She ran her fingers through her hair and added a little gloss on her lips. She had fallen in love with the hairstyle Tee had done months ago, and had stuck with it. It was just so easy and carefree. The change she made was the hue of color they had decided on. Tee had decided to make it lighter.

Fantasy removed her phone from the nightstand. She went into her voice mail, but didn't recognize the incoming number. She put the phone to her ear and listened. It was Victor. His voice sounded really weak, but it was him.

"Fantasy, I know I should have called sooner, but I didn't know how to fix us again. I can't stop thinking about you and I just wanted you to know that I love you. A friend once told me that even when she wasn't reaching out to me, she was still loving me. Fantasy, I'm still loving you." He hung up.

Fantasy sat down and listened to the message again, closer this time. By the fifth time, she realized that the noise in the background sounded like he was in a hospital. That didn't make sense to her. He was supposed to be at Andrews, unless he had gone back to Germany. The call made her smile. She didn't want to get carried away by just a call, but she felt better than she had in eleven weeks, five days, ten hours, and two minutes.

"Oh, Nick. I'm ready for my walk."

It had taken Kameron a minute to get up the courage to physically go and see Victor. Brittany had actually done the legwork and found out that he was on what they called TDY at Andrews. But, whenever she called to reach him, he was never there. It was like pulling teeth; no one would tell her anything. They had thought about asking Fantasy for the cell number, but didn't want her to get involved. So they did the next best thing, they called Nick.

They were to meet at Café Taj, an Indian restaurant in Tyson's Corner. Victor had spent almost all of his evenings and the days that he didn't have dialysis in that area. It was the place where he and Fantasy had spent the best week of his life. He had even visited the zoo three times. One of those times, he sat next to the same clown and watched him entertain the kids for hours. He visited the same stores, ate at the same places, and did some of the same things, hoping and praying that he would feel close to her; hoping that the hole in his heart would heal just a little. It didn't, and he was still lonely.

He was trying to do what he could to take care of himself, trying to stay upbeat and positive, and doing all that the doctors were telling him. They continuously told him it was necessary for his health. He was at the point of telling them that it had nothing to do with the illness or lack of rest. He was simply suffering from a broken heart. They were doctors, but maybe they were not trained to recognize matters of the heart.

When Victor heard from Kameron, he was elated. He was as nervous on the phone as he had been that day at the airport. Kameron told him how his mother had shared everything and how she encouraged him to reach out. He never doubted that Fantasy loved both him and Kameron enough to do the right thing. He just wished that he had handled the whole scenario better. He lost her for the second time and he had no one to blame again but himself. He was an expert in breaking the heart of the woman he loved more than life. She had done the right thing all the way around. So, it was time to get to know Kameron.

Victor got out of his car and looked around. Kameron didn't say what he was driving. He was early, but maybe Kameron was already inside. Victor walked inside the restaurant, and once he looked around and saw that there was no sign of Kameron, he asked to be seated where he could see the door.

Before he could sit down, Kameron walked through the door. He pointed toward Victor and walked in that direction. He extended his hand. "Hello."

Victor stood up and placed his hand in Kameron's. "Great to see you again."

"You too." He was looking directly at Victor.

Victor was looking directly at Kameron and couldn't even blink. Before, it was unplanned, and this time it was planned and he felt the same butterflies. "I'm sorry, I can't help staring at you." He laughed nervously.

"I don't know how I missed it at the airport. I felt something when I touched your hand, and I realized instantly that there was something special about you. But I didn't see me in you until Mom told me." Kameron opened the menu the server handed him.

Victor followed suit by doing the same. "How did you feel about what Fantasy told you?"

"I love my mom, and I knew how hard it was for her to share with me everything that happened between you two. I admire her because she didn't have to share. If she never told me about you and she never decided it was time to uncover some painful stuff, I would not have been the wiser and life would have gone on. Mom has a good heart, even at self cost."

The server returned. "You ready to order?" The lady stood positioned with pen to pad, ready to take their request.

"I'll have the ginger chicken and vegetable pakoras," Kameron responded, and handed her the menu.

"I'll have the same." Victor decided just to make it simple. He wasn't trying to show their similarities or anything, but the sooner he ordered, the sooner he could hand his menu to her and she would be on her way, leaving them alone.

"I know that you know a lot about me, but I don't feel like I know anything about you except what everyone else knows. So, I'm all ears if that's what you want to talk about, and if it's not I will listen to whatever you have to say."

Kameron smiled. "First off, you can call me Kam. Everyone in my family does and I happen to like the nickname."

"Okay, Kam it is then."

"We should just let things flow. If you want to ask me something in particular, shoot. I'm easy to get along with. But I don't want this to be formal. I believe we have a long time to get to know each other. Now, I realize that a lot of time has been lost, but it is what it is. My belief is that we make the best of it."

"I'm with you there," Victor said. "I'll tell you what, why don't I clear the air on one major issue that affects both of us?" He took a sip of the Masala tea that had been brought out a few minutes earlier.

"What's that?" Kam took a sip of his and leaned forward on his elbows to listen to him.

"I love your mother. I've loved her for a lifetime. Losing her and making the crazy decision to marry Sonya was the biggest mistake of my life. From day one all your mother did was love me. She was aware that I had a girlfriend, and, because I was going through some drama, she provided a shoulder. She never had a hidden agenda, she never talked bad about Sonya, she just extended her friendship. Not many women can do that. It was so easy to fall in love with her. To know that I had another chance to do the right thing and messed it up is tearing me apart. She deserves so much and it seems in one way or the other all I do is bring her drama and heartache." Victor felt himself tear up. He didn't mind being emotional, but he wasn't ready to be all emotional in front of his son. He wanted to come across as a little hard with just a touch of sensitivity.

Kam was looking at Victor and he blinked a few times. Is this brother tearing up? he thought. "It's my job to protect her. That's what I've always done and that's what I will always do. Even if it means protecting her from you. We can have a relationship. I'm cool with that. But if you being in my mom's life is not good, I'm not having it." Kam paused.

Victor looked stunned. He shouldn't have been; this guy was going to school to be a lawyer, all the more reason why he should be direct and forceful with an edge. On top of that, he was their son and both of them were direct and no nonsense. He was proud, even though he was getting put in his place by his son. "I'm not—"

"Please, let me finish. I believe you love my mom; there's no denying that from all she has shared, and I know that she is madly in love with you. The two of you are miserable without each other. You need to go after your woman. You let her get away one time for twenty-one years. I don't think you got another twenty-one in you. But if I were you, I wouldn't let another day pass by without letting her know."

"You are right. I'm going to Charlotte." Victor wiped the tears away. He couldn't believe that his son had just straightened him out. He was wise beyond his years.

"You've got to go a little farther than Charlotte. Mom's in Jamaica with Nick. She needed some post-surgery R and R. Not to mention she's trying to mend her heart."

"Oh, God, is she okay?" Fantasy had not mentioned anything previously. So he was trying to figure out if something new had occurred or if there had been an accident.

"She had back surgery." Kam thanked the server who placed his food in front of him. "And, please, man up. All this crying just doesn't work for my image. If you're going to hang with me and I'm going to be introducing you to people as my dad, you may need to keep it together." Kam started laughing. He hoped that Victor could stand jokes, because that was part of his personality.

He was touched again by what Kam had said. "I'll do my best. You are your mom's son." And already he could see himself in the young man that sat across from him, assertive and totally in control. Not quite as emotional, but Kameron was a part of him.

"So, what's it going to be?" Kam had started eating.

"Can you get away for a few days?" Victor looked at Kam.

"Possibly. What's up?" He didn't understand.

"We are going to Jamaica," Victor said.

Kam slapped him five. "My old dude."

Chapter 21

Fantasy was reading through the messages that Victor had written. The next evening after she received the voice mail he called back. He talked and she listened. It was hard to get back on the bike, but there was right and wrong on both their parts. She would love to say that she held no blame in any of it, but she had. She reflected on what she had said to Kam at the family dinner. For all that time she'd never realized how all of it tied together and how very much she was affected by her mom. That day wasn't just for Kam, it was for her. She need to understand all the ways so she could move on and not be held hostage by the things that would so easily entangle her and cause her to lose her mind.

Feeling the need to do something she hadn't done in a while, she looked around for her laptop. Once she spied it, she moved gingerly across the room, picked it up, and brought it back to the bed. Getting comfortable, she placed a few pillows behind her back and one under her knees. She signed on to her Facebook account and began a message to Victor:

It's been a minute since I've sent you a message just to let you know how much I love you. Today I realized how special all of our time has been, and even the time when we are far apart and somehow our hearts are so intertwined, we are still together. That's why at this very mo-

ment I feel so close to you. When I lay in your arms listening to your heartbeat, I smiled because each beat mimicked my heartbeat perfectly. I am in awe of us and how perfect two people could be for one another, and knowing that those two people are you and I. It's as if I breathe in, knowing that exhaling will find me more in love with you than the moment before. I hope you don't mind me being this deep. For months I've been walking around hurt and holding on to stuff that I should have let go. Not until today did I realize that it was because I was not your number one. And even in the now, even right this moment, to take all that I'm feeling and stand at the playing board and put everything on us frightens me, because it might mean that in my mind, in my soul, and in my heart of hearts you have been my number one and although I bared my soul and opened up you didn't accept what I had to offer. What a woman I've always been, knowing when to walk away and somehow being able to pick up the pieces and hope. Then one day I just stopped hoping. I figured that it was better to just let someone love me and pray that I was it for them, without unveiling what I really needed, what I really wanted. I took only what was offered and made it enough. I never felt abundant love was for me. So there are days I hold back, and, honestly, days I hide behind my work, when I just don't want to hurt again. The times when we have been together and it's time for you to leave, my heart breaks. You've seen those tears, so can you even imagine me having to let you go again? And yet I know that you have grown and I know you feel bad and I even believe you love me more than you ever thought possible. There is a future for us. I feel in my heart that you are my forever, and I'm going to love you harder, better, deeper, and longer than any you've ever known. Every morning you will wake up to my smile; you will be touched with the softness of my caress; throughout each day you will be reminded that you have a partner, a mate, an intercessor, and a burden-sharer; and at night you will rest in the arms of your lover, your friend, and your wife. As we wait for night to completely capture the day we will make love and merge our souls together in a place where there is nothing but our love, and the distance between is no more than a thin vapor of air. You are my forever. Love, Fantasy

Fantasy had noticed that someone from her job had sent her a Facebook friend request. By the time she'd answered it, she'd gotten a message back from Victor:

Your words melted my heart. I love you so very, very much, Fantasy, and although we took the long way back to each other (my fault), you indeed are my soul mate and I thank God for you every day. You are my future. Everything that I see and feel from this moment forward has you, has me, has "Us." I promise to spend the rest of my life demonstrating how special you are to and for me. I can't wait. It's the little things we will do together that will have the biggest impact on me. They already have! God showed me my mistake many years ago. I will never lose you or your love for me again. I love you, and I am deeply in love with you. You are my forever. Love, Victor

Fantasy read the message twice and was so touched. She went back and looked at their first communication:

This is a very distant blast from your past. I'm a very old friend from your college days. You likely don't even remember me, although I'd like to think we have a little history and I at least made a lasting impression. I really don't know what I expect or if I should expect anything, not even a response. I was looking at a page of one of your fraternity brothers, an old friend as well, and there you were. What a wonder this social network is; I just haven't determined if it's a good one or a bad one. I'm totally new to this, and I'm sure after a while I'll be able to decide. My intent tonight was to reach out and say hello for old time's sake. I hope all is well, Fantasy

Yes, this is definitely a blast from the past, and a very pleasant one. I do remember you, Fantasy. I must admit, when I saw your message I looked out my window, thinking you had someone posted outside my house ready to take me out. You see, in remembering, I also remember the hurt I caused you. It was long ago, true, but nevertheless a period of time that I have not forgotten. I was young and dumb, and I handled "us" badly. For what it's worth, I'm so very sorry. Even now that doesn't seem like enough. I know my apology is coming some twenty years later, and I wish that weren't the case. Walking away from you was the hardest thing I ever had to do, and for all these years it has haunted me. Somehow I knew our paths would cross again and I'd have a chance to make amends, or at least try. A young man is too naïve to fix what he messes up, and an older man cares so much about mending what's broken it is all he can think about. There was no way I could ever forget. Fantasy, if you will let me, I'd like to keep in touch with you. I just want the opportunity to say and do what I should have so long ago. Forever! Victor

She just needed to look back at how they started all over again. Just then, she saw another message come through from Victor. As she waited for the page to open, she noticed that the sun was going down and it was picture perfect outside. She had never seen something so beautiful, and she was eager to go out on the balcony and watch it descend over the water.

Fantasy, why don't you come and take a walk with me? Victor

She jumped up and pushed the laptop to the side. She spoke out loud. "What in the world is he talking about?"

She yelled for Nick, who was in the next room, and got no answer. She walked slowly through the house and didn't see him anywhere. Maybe he's outside. Just as she walked through the door, she saw Nick standing close to the front step with a smile. She was getting ready to fuss at him when she looked up and, from a distance, she saw Victor walking toward the villa.

She covered her mouth and tears began to flow. Kam came up behind her out of nowhere and handed her a tissue. "It's okay, I'm sure he's crying too."

She walked down the steps and across the sand with bare feet. The sun was positioned over the water, giving her time to reach her destination. It wanted to create the ideal backdrop for the love that existed between the two old lovers. When she got to him she didn't know what to say.

Victor reached for her hand and slowly kissed each finger. Just as Kam had said, there were tears. He marveled at how beautiful she was, and he spoke from his heart. He knew that they were going to try again, and this time he'd work harder. He realized the gamble she was taking, and it was all in the name of love. How could he even begin to tell her?

"I'm not waiting another moment. I love you and I want you to marry me." Victor reached into his pocket and pulled out a box.

"Yes." Fantasy giggled and kissed him until her head began to spin.

"Aren't you going to look at your ring?" Victor held her tight, but not too tight.

"I don't need to. But first things first. Nick told me about the dialysis."

Victor looked down. He was going to share that with her, but he'd wanted the happiness first. "I was going to tell—"

"Shh. I knew something was wrong when I first saw you again in DC. We are going to get you well and then I'm going to become Mrs. Victor Charles." Fantasy smiled up at Victor, who was the love of her life.

"You don't mind waiting?" Victor asked.

"I've never stopped loving you and I love you still." Fantasy kissed Victor again and held on tight, not wanting anything to interrupt their moment.

"Thank you for taking the chance," Victor whispered in her ear as the wind blew across the sands.

Notes

Notes